The Church of Solitude

SUNY series, Women Writers in Translation
Marilyn Gaddis Rose, editor

The Church of Solitude

Grazia Deledda

Translated by E. Ann Matter

State University of New York Press

This translation is based on the first edition of *La chiesa della solitudine* (Milan: Treves, 1936). © 1936, by Grazia Deledda. Permission to publish is gratefully acknowledged to Alessandro Madesani-Deledda, on behalf of the Estate of Grazia Deledda.

Published by
State University of New York Press, Albany

For information, address State University of New York Press,
90 State Street, Suite 700, Albany, NY 12207

Production by Marilyn P. Semerad
Marketing of Anne M. Valentine

Library of Congress Cataloging-in-Publication Data

Deledda, Grazia, 1871–1936.
    [Chiesa della solitudine. English]
    The church of solitude / Grazia Deledda ; translated by E. Ann Matter.
      p. cm.
    ISBN 0-7914-5457-6 (hc : acid free)—ISBN 0-7914-5458-4 (pb : acid free)
      I. Matter, E. Ann. II. Title.

PQ4811.E6 C4513 2002
853'.8—dc21   2002020092

10 9 8 7 6 5 4 3 2 1

The Church
of
Solitude

Maria Concezione left the small hospital of her town on the seventh of December, the vigil of her saint's day. She had undergone a serious operation: her left breast had been completely cut away. Upon discharging her, the head physician had said with Olympian and crystalline cruelty, "You are fortunate you are no longer very young—twenty-eight, I believe—so the disease will take some time to come back. Ten years, maybe even twelve. In any case, take good care of yourself. Don't overwork. Don't seek out emotion. Peace and quiet, right? And let me see you every now and again."

She looked at him with great black eyes in the lean, tarnished face of a fallen angel. She would have liked to have made little horns with her fingers, or some other sign of exorcism; but deep down she didn't believe in those things, and for a long time now she had been resigned to her fate. It was quite enough for her to resolve to never return to the hospital again.

Now she was going home, all wrapped up and encased in a long black shawl that made her tall body seem more slender, and her Bedouin profile even darker. She brushed past the wall of the hospital garden, and then past the lower wall of a garden planted almost entirely with cabbages with great lunar flowers. She came out immediately onto a country road, rutted and stony, that led towards the nearby mountains. Everything seemed different from the way she had left it. She herself was different, empty, and, it seemed to her, with the smell of death on her clothes, a smell that would never leave her again.

And yet she was happy: to walk, to breathe, to be hungry, to love her mother, her house, even her cat. The joy of living.

For days, after a long drought, it had rained abundantly. The earth was black, so much so that in some places it seemed to be sprinkled with coffee grounds. But from the sides of the road, between the two inclines that gradually sloped down to the Valley of the Birchi and the Valley of the Capro, two small streams engorged by the torrents and brought back to life by the recent rains, the masses of almost silvery granite stood out even better, speckled with black sparks that seemed like reefs in the midst of long, wet, dark, algaelike vegetation. It all had something of the bottom of the sea about it, from the swell of the valley and the sudden wave of the landscape, as if the sea in some ancient time had arrived as far as the foot of the mountains and the elevation out of which the town arose. The very mountains above Concezione's house had the arid, rocky look of an indented, corroded coastline that had once been beaten by waves. Only higher up were they blackened by the ancient oak forests.

The house where she stopped was also unusual. It stood at a fork in the road that climbed up the slope of the mountain on one side, and on the other led down to the valley on the left. It was a small church, with a façade that in fact looked down into the valley, and was surrounded on the front and one side by a clearing marked by a little hedge enclosing a garden with fruit trees, a little wooden gate that opened, and a path leading to the eastern side of the church, which was used as a dwelling.

Only two little windows fortified with iron grilles opened from the wall of the old building, where the road turned under the clearing. One roof of black tile, encrusted with moss and its parasitic plants, covered both the church and the house. Two markers, two symbols looked down from one corner to the other, over the two valleys of the promontory; they looked down like brothers who, though far away and separated by a whole world, remember each other tenderly, being sons of the same mother. Rising above the façade, on top of a small arch from which hung a bell, was a cross; on the side of the garden and almost over the door to the house, was a chimney out of which came a banner of smoke that gladdened Concezione's heart. She made the sign of the cross before opening the little gate, and cleaned her feet on the grass, almost as though she wanted to leave outside the dust and memory of the ugly places and sad days she had gone through. Her joy was heartfelt when her mother appeared at the little door of the house—a small figure, hard and all gray, as though part of the colors and the nature of the rocks around her; but just like the granite, she had a silvery clarity, an odd mixture of the joyous and the solemn.

She had not expected her daughter's return so soon and was not elated to see her. She knew she would come back, that the little Madonna of the church watched over the two of them and would not betray them. So her large mouth crowned by silver hairs barely smiled as she finished drying her hands on her gray apron. And Concezione, after a nod of greeting, walked through the kitchen to put away her shawl in a chest in the next room. The aroma of quinces came out of the chest full of clothes. A large bed, with a blanket of hand-woven wool, all embroidered with flowers and birds of red and blue, took up almost all of the room and served both of the women. The bed was so high that underneath it were stored baskets and tools, rolls of spun wool, a sack of potatoes and a smaller one of beans, but everything on the pavement of rough red tile was clean and in order. In a basket full of carded wool lay the beautiful black cat who looked as if he had put on a furry white nightcap to sleep better. He opened one green eye, looked at his mistress, and went back to sleep, participating in the Olympian tranquillity of the place. But returning to the kitchen, Concezione flushed with irritation to see that her mother had taken a dead suckling pig with a red rind out of the cupboard against the wall; its belly was cut open and stuffed with myrtle branches. Her mother looked at it with uncertainty and a bit of disquiet, and seemed to speak to it.

"Poor little beast probably only three days old. Well!"

She sighed, resigning herself to the destiny of the tiny victim. In the end, one should always be happy when Providence sends gifts. Her still youthful voice went on, "Aroldo came last night. He brought this for you—for your celebration. He'll come back tonight. He wanted to go to the hospital, but I advised against it. He seemed very happy, just the same. So, what shall we do with this little beast?"

"Do whatever you want. He'll eat it," she said scornfully. "He didn't have to bring it."

"But Concezione!"

Her mother looked her full in the face, and only then did she realize that her daughter was completely changed. She seemed to have aged all at once, with withered skin surrounding her dark eyes, and hair pulled back against her temples and tied tight on her neck just like an old woman. And she thought that, yes, Aroldo was too young for her. He was still a boy, good and in love, yes, but not one to think of as a possible husband. Besides, he was of a different breed than theirs; even his language was so different that the old woman understood his words with difficulty. But from his blue eyes, from his luminous smile, and from his warm voice she understood his loyalty and gentleness, and she loved him like a child. Concezione had also never been hostile towards him, quite the contrary; but now the illness had changed her.

They spoke about this illness as little as possible, like a mysterious thing. Even its terrible name, that not even the doctors had pronounced clearly, remained deep in their hearts with a secret agreement to never reveal it, not even to themselves. So, Concezione didn't tell her mother what the head physician of the hospital had said to her. She only said, as her mother quickly handed her a cup of coffee, that she felt very weak and shouldn't wear herself out.

"Yes," she said as if following her mother's thoughts, "I am changed; I feel old, but tranquil. I'll take up my work again and we'll live happily."

Her work was easy: she sewed linens, especially men's clothing. This was how she knew Aroldo, who last summer had asked her to make six shirts for him.

But before sitting down between the window and the fire with her work basket next to her, she went into the church, passing through the small sacristy that opened onto the kitchen. The little room had a small, high window that opened towards the north. It framed the mountain like a melancholy painting without a background of sky, and the crude light of the bare rocks gave it a profound sense of glacial solitude. The church, entered through a short hall from the little sacristy, also seemed to be carved out of the earth, it was so cold and humid. The gleam of the small lamps next to the altar, and of the dusty lunette over the door increased its sadness. But with the window open, in the blue light from the horizon clearing over the distant valley, the poor sanctuary seemed less icy and desolate. Nothing adorned it. The roof was of planks, just like a cabin. A stone bench along the wall served for a seat. But the single altar covered with an embroidered cloth, the long and precious work of Concezione, was almost rich. Ten gilded glass candelabra with thick candles like a staircase, five on each side, gave wings to the small wooden statute of the Madonna of Solitude.

This little, almost proud Madonna seemed ready to defy the most arctic and boundless solitude, all dark and rigid in her blue niche spotted with damp that gave the impression of a marine grotto, the kind that appears through the clouds in the torn sky of a tempestuous evening. In fact, the sliver of moon supporting the feet of the brown statue was the only serene touch to sweeten the severity. Even the Child, whom her long, slack hands held a bit low as if to slip them within the wrinkled folds of her dress, was sulky, snub-nosed, bestial; but his fat little feet, rebellious and agitated, his toes sticking out, his big toes almost alive, gave even him a sense of tenderness, of almost joyous humanity. Concezione gazed at these little feet rather that at the Madonna, hard and absent, truly all alone above the moon.

Then she relit the little lamp, moved the vase of dusty and faded paper flowers, and finally kneeled down with a shiver of cold down her back.

Her soul also trembled with cold, with sadness, with fear— a sudden fear of life, of days awaiting her all alike, always alike, without either love or hope. And those holy little feet up there, in the reddish light like twilight before nightfall, gave her a deep longing for tears.

"I should not have children; I shouldn't have any," she thought, among the words of her prayer, "and it's right, it's right. Everything in your will is right, O Lord. I have sinned against love, I have sown pain and destroyed a man's life; and now you sprinkle the salt of sterility on my life, O Lord. Thy will be done. And you, Virgin Mother, help me now to get through this desolate life of mine. Look down on me from the heights of your mercy."

And it seemed that help was not lacking during the hours of that day, gray and still like the surrounding rocks. Seated in front of her work basket full of a roll of pink cotton for men's shirts, she tried to make buttonholes on cuffs already basted before she went into the hospital. But she was weak, her left arm still numb; still, in comparison to the sad days she had just spent, she felt she had returned to a luminous palace, and that the view out of the window—the garden clearing, the bushes, the boulders of the embankment—was a spring garden. A joy of life overcame her in spite of herself. It was a humble rhythm: the purring of the cat curled up on the stones of the hearth, the aroma of the suckling pig her mother had put to roast in the oven where she occasionally made bread, and the silent coming and going of her mother, intent upon the household chores. The same immobile silence was outside, broken only by the occasional wheels of a cart or the passing of a horse on the country road.

But towards evening the solitude came alive: a man's figure, disproportionate and jarring in the scheme of that poor, amazed scene, loomed large among the small things of the kitchen. It was Aroldo, the foreigner. He carried on his back a type of knapsack which he took slowly from his sturdy arms and set in a corner, pushing away the suddenly curious and greedy cat with the palm of his hand.

"Go away, you rascal," he said, petting him. "Isn't the good smell in here enough for you?"

And he himself sniffed the air, like a guest come to a place of well-being and rest. But the black figure of Concezione, with that dark face and eyes laden with shadows, seemed to darken his own. The smile faded from his mouth, a beautiful mouth, with the shiny lips of an infant and teeth which still seemed like milk teeth.

The rest of him was also handsome, almost too highly colored: ruddy face, blond hair, blue eyes with dark eyebrows, high and arched like those of a woman, made more alive and sweet. His strong neck was red, red his strong hands, all strong, alive, full-blooded, in his almost gigantic body.

And yet, he seemed to pale and shrink, as if trying to hide inside the breadth of his rough-spun clothing for Concezione's unexpected welcome. He saw the change clearly—she neither displayed it nor hid it; she seemed another person to him too. It was as if the hospital, instead of the operation the two women had described to him—that is, the simple extraction of a nasal polyp—had by witchcraft taken her blood, her flesh, her youth. Something inexplicable, beyond the breath of sorrow and illness, emanated from her, almost a sense of threat and danger, chilling the comforting, hospitable atmosphere of the house. He felt like he was once again the stranger, like that day when he came carrying the material for his shirts and Concezione had taken his measurements without looking him in the face: a stranger from a distant land, without a soul in the world. But with those measurements, Concezione had bound him, bewitched him; and those shirts she had sewn were to him a boy's new clothes, party clothes, a thread of hope and joy.

"How are you doing?" he asked in a low, troubled voice. He seemed to be afraid of being overheard by someone who was more the master of the house than the owners themselves, someone who could throw him out like an intruder.

"Sit down. Fine. Everything's fine," said the mother. "Concezione is cured: you see her."

"I see her," he said, but uncertainly, not daring to address himself directly to the young woman. In fact, he took two steps back towards the door, waiting for her to decide to come towards him; he was ready to leave if she ordered it. Aware of this, she wore a smile between mockery and pity.

"So sit down," she said, almost rudely, patting the back of a chair next to the hearth. "Where are you coming from?"

Red from emotion and joy, he gestured toward the door with his arm. He had come from far away, down there, from the place where this valley joins with another valley that little by little grows bigger, becomes almost a plain, and slopes down to the sea. He was building a provincial road down there, a road that came up from the coast towards the town of the two women. Aroldo, with other workers from across the sea, led by a manager who was also a foreigner, worked on the construction of this road, especially of the bridges.

"Then what's new?" demanded the old woman, while Concezione made a to-do about setting the table, on which already lay a platter full of pieces of the suckling pig, giving off the good aroma of rosemary.

Seeing those preparations, Aroldo began again to brighten. These women had already invited him other times, and, with his appetite awakened by the long walk, he felt especially happy about their hospitality that evening.

"News? What news could I bring? We work like slaves, and the boss is always there yelling and pushing us around. Never happy. And on top of that, with all these rains, the ground is bad. There are small landslides and water running everywhere. But where there's a will there's a way. Anyway, the boss likes me, maybe because I'm the hardest worker. So . . . " He looked at Concezione's back and did not continue. His face grew dark again.

But when they were at the table and the old woman poured out his drink, even though the wine was light pink like a soft drink, he took courage. Eating slowly, using his fork and knife like a gentleman, he once again began to tell in his lightly cadenced voice stories of the road and the manager.

"He's a character, though. He's already been to America twice, building roads and bridges, and now he really has a plan in mind. You have to admit that he's a great worker. He lives with us and spends the nights with us in the camp. He doesn't even go back to town on Sunday, like we laborers are allowed to do. For one thing, he wants us to go to mass; in fact, I certainly wouldn't tramp all that long way if not for mass . . . "

Concezione understood perfectly that he returned only for her, but she remained rigid and hard. She did not eat, she did not move from the table as her mother did every now and again. She was absent, though, and seemed not to hear the words of the guest. She only started, almost in spite of herself, when he continued,

"And now this is what's happening: yes, but I'm only telling you because it shouldn't be known, at least not for awhile. So, today the manager called me to one side and asked me if I want to go to America with him as soon as this road is finished, that is, in a year or so. It seems that this time he has really big plans. Not only does he want to open a road in an unexplored forest towards Patagonia, but even to build a city, and then a branch of the railroad. Like I say, the place is uninhabited now, but within two or three years it will certainly be magnificent, with completely new houses, very fertile land, vegetable and flower gardens, fountains. It will be a lot of work you understand, but there will also be a lot to gain: maybe riches, certainly a good future."

The old woman forced herself to understand, but it all seemed a bit of a fairy tale, a bit of a joke, especially since, when he was in a good mood, Aroldo never hesitated to tell her tall tales. But he contented himself with playing jokes on the mother since the daughter was too quick and too distrustful to be taken in by him.

But this time he was serious and committed, and maybe his story was not a fantasy. So Concezione listened, without showing it, to his every word, with a mixture of curiosity and hope.

Here's how the Virgin of Solitude had somehow heard her prayer: if Aroldo were to go, she would be once again completely alone and free on the road that fate had laid out before her. Her mother's question even made her smile: "But who's going down there to make this new country? You and the manager?"

"And hundreds and hundreds of fellows, some from here, some natives. First of all we'll make a sort of colony, with little houses for us; then a true cooperative, with a just division of profits. The better you are, the more you work, the bigger part of the enterprise you'll have. And insurance to cover work, illness, misfortunes, life; and even full freedom to come back, with compensation for work and for the trip. The climate is good. There aren't any dangerous beasts. A lot of insects, yes, especially mosquitoes, but they disappear as soon as the land is drained."

"And the money?" Concezione scoffed, mocking him.

"I think the manager has it. He isn't a fool, and he doesn't talk just to talk. He's a bit odd, it's true, but he's ambitious and passionate about these things. Anyway, there's nothing to lose, at least not for someone like me."

He also struck a mocking pose, but against himself. He drank another glass of wine, pushed back the plate which the old woman had refilled, and looked up straight ahead, as if he saw a painting that interested him more than the other things around him. He went on, "Certainly I won't be the one to be afraid of the mosquitoes, not even of snakes, if there are any. When I was a boy I killed many snakes, even some poisonous ones. My mother and I lived in a worse cabin than those we'll go live in 'down there.' The poor woman worked in the rice fields until she died from hardships, but she still sent me to school and dreamed of a happy future for me. After she died I worked first as a knife sharpener. I had a boss then too, a blind man who had only his sharpening machine and who went around with me and controlled my work more than even the engineer will control it in that new city 'down there.' We went from one place to another; there was work especially in the summer: scythes, scissors, axes, and knives for the women who make pasta at home and cut salami in thin pieces for youngsters. They slipped us a few pieces too, with a bit of polenta, on those threshing floors, bless them. People are good up there, but in the rice fields they are also poor; there was a lot of misery there. We slept wherever we ended up; it was then that I learned to catch snakes and to toughen my skin against mosquitoes. Once we happened to be in a town where a house had burned down. The owner wanted to rebuild it at once, while the weather was still good, and scraped together all the available workers in town. But almost all of them were busy because they were building a dike; and so I was offered work as a laborer. The owner of the burned house and my boss argued over me. I was tired of the vagabond life and the abuses of the knife sharpener, who often left me without food. Then a strange thing happened. The wife of the house had known my mother because she had also been in the rice fields as a girl. Not only that, but she told me she had known the man who, according to her, had deceived and then abandoned my mother. A gentleman, she said, one of those who inspected the work in the rice fields. I thought all the time about this unknown scoundrel, my father. My mother had never talked about him to me, not even on her deathbed, so I had thought I was an orphan. Now my fantasies were kindled, and it was this illusion that made me decide to abandon the knife sharpener and take up a career as a laborer. Those certainly were hard times. For all the research I could do, I wasn't able to find out anything about my father. When the house was done, I found something to do with the work on the dike. Then a worker took me with him to work on a railroad. He also paid me little, but I learned the trade, especially how to work on bridges and escarpments, and as they say, I managed. Now I am here, then maybe I'll go down there in America. And, then . . . anyway, I've already told you my story. There is no shame in being nobody's son; I live by my own work and I don't have any illusions."

It seemed he really wanted to explain about his mother's past and his vagabond life. He knew that the town of his hostesses didn't have much esteem for the children of sin, especially if they were poor. But he did not wish to deceive anyone, and since Concezione had already shown him an attachment not lacking warmth, there was no reason why she should change her mind all at once.

After all, he thought that she also made her living from her meager work, in that strange refuge, half holy and half outlaw, inherited, in fact, from ancestors who, public opinion assured him, were little if at all scrupulous in terms of honesty. As he spoke, she seemed to get back some of her former cordiality. She smiled again, this time benevolently, when her mother asked with naive cunning whether there would also be women "down there" to help and console the pioneers.

"Not at first, I think. We'll go live in barracks, alone, like castaways. But as soon as the houses are ready, the manager will be the first to want women with us. They're necessary for many reasons."

A smile that wanted to be mischievous carved out the dimples of his cheeks, and the blue of his eyes became all golden. He looked at Concezione, and she repeated his words as if to humor him: "Yes, for many reasons."

Now he looked up again at that painting which only he saw.

"Certainly, it will be hard at first, but like I say, I'm used to it. I'm strong," he said, stretching out his arms with his fists closed. "I'll be at the head of the line and the boss knows it well. At any rate, we'll arrive there just at the beginning of the good weather, and so it won't be hard for us men to camp out like soldiers. In fact, it's a life that does you good. And then we'll be provided with everything, even with wine, coffee, medicine. The manager promises that there will even be a doctor, but on the other hand he will only hire men who are healthy and more than capable. Once the first houses are built, once the bad weather is over, then he'll think about bringing women."

"But, how will they do it? Alone?"

It was again the mother who inquired, even though by now she was also disenchanted with the story.

"Oh yes, why not? There are wives and sisters of emigrants who want nothing better than to join them. You go where God helps you to live, and no one says that you have to live in a strange land forever. If a woman wants to go down there she can be sent the money for the trip and she can be met at the dock, which isn't far. Rather, the hard part will be the trip into the interior if the railroad hasn't reached our colony yet."

"Good luck!" said Concezione, recovering her amused tone. "I certainly won't go!"

The words were said. It was a light cut, but like a furtive but sure blow, it neatly divided the destiny dreamed of by Aroldo: he was on one side with his fantastic city, and on the other side was Concezione in her cave. The painting disappeared from her wall. He blinked his dark lashes lightly over his darkened eyes. His mouth looked like the mouth of a child who refuses his medicine. He himself hardly believed his courage and his voice asking, "And if you were my wife?"

These words upset the mother as well. Her placid eyes ran from one young face to the other, and she didn't even know herself what she wanted: was it an affirmative answer from Concezione or her definitive rejection of the young suitor's dream?

Concezione, her head bowed, seemed to think before proclaiming her decision, and then she said calmly, "That's just talk!"

Then there was still hope. Now the old woman, who knew with ancient wisdom how just one word could sometimes influence the destiny of others, thought she should not intervene with her advice. Instead, with the excuse of going to get something from the bedroom, she got up and left the two young people alone.

Slowly, Aroldo stretched out his hand and placed it on Concezione's. She didn't pull hers back, but stolidly hid the burning commotion that the contact gave her.

He said softly, "Remember one night, there in the garden, we kissed; and you promised to marry me as soon as my position would allow it. My position will certainly get better as soon as I am down there—if I go that's what I'll go for. I'm not asking you to follow me, not until I also have kept my promise; but you should promise to wait for me. Two years, only two years of your time . . . "

She smiled, that sad, tired, but still ironic smile that left her teeth uncovered all the way to her slightly discolored gums. She took back her hand, slipping it from his like a cat, and answered out loud, since she no longer had anything to hide, "In two years I will be old; in fact, I'm already old and sick. I'm no longer good for anything—and you are young, Aroldo; you need a strong, healthy woman to follow you and help you make your fortune wherever you are."

"I need you, Concezione. I don't know why, but from the moment I met you, I have felt that only you could make me happy, and that God had sent me to this place to meet you. I can't live without you anymore. Even if I go to the ends of the earth, even if I become a millionaire, I will always think about you. But why should I go to the ends of the earth to seek my fortune if you don't love me anymore? Everything would be useless without you. I prefer to stay here and be miserable; and if you throw me out I will return to your door like a beggar. You don't send beggars away."

He spoke clearly and well, with his even, cadenced voice that came from a sincere heart. It seemed like a song: resigned, but with an inexorable passion that creates light for itself, one of those songs of hopeless love that Concezione had heard and learned from her earliest adolescence. Indeed, those songs were the accompaniment, almost the cause, of her first restlessness, of her curiosity and sensual turmoil. It was not the first time that Aroldo had spoken to her like this: his first declarations of love had sounded the same, and she had let herself be conquered as if by a music that recalls bygone things and makes them come alive again. A reflowering of sensations, impulses, but also of illusions, had pulled her close to him. Next to his youth that seemed poor but was actually very rich, his manly warmth, the controlled but profound exuberance of his vitality, she felt like those herbs and those mean wildflowers that, in the presence of herbs and flowers richer than they are, take on, if nothing else, the appearance of others. And then, besides the physical desire, the natural rush of her flesh towards his, she was attracted by the very difference of breed, of age, of character, of language. It seemed like this should distance them, but instead it pushed them more towards each other.

In the hut where, for a few lire, Aroldo rented a hole in the wall to stay on his days off, they had told him that Concezione was descended from a line of violent and passionate people, and that she herself had suffered a tragic passion during her early girlhood. Knowing that he frequented her house, they did not go into details. But he was fixed in his ideas: he wanted Concezione, at all costs he wanted her. The very atmosphere that surrounded her, between the romantic and the ambiguous, seemed to awaken a type of fever in his blood, tormenting him with a sting that wounded his heart, and, even more, his senses. He wanted Concezione: day and night he longed for her. One look from her eye to his was enough to give him almost a desire for possession, a delirium that exalted him and rendered him mute.

But now it was all finished. She didn't look at him anymore; she had become another person. He really did have the impression that the hospital had changed her, turning her into an empty, old, ghostly Concezione.

"I know," he said, thinking over the stories they had told him about her, "you never really loved me; and if I go far away you'll forget me easily; you'll even find another man."

"There's no danger of that, Aroldo!" she said, frowning, since she knew what he was getting at. "I will always stay here with my mother and the little Madonna. And we will die here, God willing. Oh yes, God wills it, since we have faith in him; and nobody can ever hurt me again."

As if comforted, he continued, "Then so be it. But tell me, what if I am able to come back in two years, maybe three, and take you both away, both you and your mother? What do you say, Giustina?"

The old woman had come back in with a tray and cups; she placed them on the table and poured the coffee. She was tranquil, and in the light of the oil lamp, her smooth face seemed younger than Concezione's. She set a cup down before the young man and said, "Dear son, your words are pretty, but they are like a puff of wind that starts the branches rustling and then stops."

Irritated, but respectful, he replied, "Let's see now, what have you understood?"

"I understand, I understand. You want to uproot the boulder above our garden and make it roll to the bottom of the valley. But is that ever possible?"

"Oh, if we are going to speak in parables, it's useless to continue. Look, this is the way things stand: I have been offered the possibility of making a decent fortune. I am offering to share this good luck with Concezione and you. If you don't want to follow me, at least Concezione could wait for me for two years."

"But why do you repeat these things to her?" asked Concezione with irritation, "I have already answered. I am not a child, and I don't like useless talk!"

Aroldo blushed to his neck and did not dare insist; but a furtive glance from the mother seemed to say to him, "Let some time go by; you'll see that things will change."

Then there was a knock on the door, and she went to open it with neither surprise nor curiosity. A man appeared whose size took up all the space of the small opening. He was old, but he had a giant head surrounded by a thick beard down to his throat, a mixture of black, white, and reddish. His face was like a satyr's mask, with a large nose and the savage, golden eyes of a courageous wild boar. He wore a short cape of rough cloth, with a large hood folded back on his shoulders. He seemed to have continued growing even as an old man, since his bare wrists and boxer's hands stuck out of his sleeves. He pushed his cloth cap back a bit on his bald head and then pulled it down again on his forehead over his hairy eyebrows: that was his greeting.

Aroldo moved over, as if to give him room at the table; but once the little door was closed, the old man sat almost on top of it, on a stool too small for him. He put a hand to his hairy ear to better hear old Giustina's words of introduction.

"This is our friend, Felice Giordano; and this is our friend Aroldo."

The old man, who already knew something about the stranger, said at once in his extraordinarily sonorous, yet aggressive, voice, "He doesn't have a last name? Friends anyway," he added hastily; and with his cane he scratched the back of the cat that had immediately come to him.

This was something that made Aroldo childishly jealous, and made him care for the ruddy visitor even less, since the animal never willingly let Aroldo pet him. He said his whole name in a loud voice: "Aroldo Aroldi." But the other seemed to no longer pay any attention to him, but now concentrated all of his attention on the young hostess who, for her part, fixed him with an ironic challenge, inviting him to come closer.

"Come on, come over here with us. Drink a glass of water if you don't want anything else."

He raised his right hand with the index finger bent so that the shadow on the wall was the head of a bird of prey. He made a menacing gesture, but Concezione had no fear of him; rather, she started to laugh, and her white teeth, in her still hard face, seemed a bit cruel to Aroldo.

The mother explained, "Our Compare* Felice doesn't like coffee. Nor pork," she added, touching the plate of leftovers from the roast. To reinforce her statement, the old man turned towards the wall and spit, as his long top lip curled with comic but sincere disgust.

"Coffee is for women. The meat of pigs is for those who steal them."

"This one, at least, is not stolen," replied Concezione, to defend the now mortified gift giver.

"I don't know anything about that; I only say that pork causes bad dreams, and even the Jews don't eat it. And I am a Christian."

---

*Compare: untranslatable term of respect for a companion or accomplice with almost familial intimacy. Feminine: Comare.

"That is to say, he has two hundred pigs. Every year he sells more than one hundred nice fat ones, fed on the acorns from his woods on the mountain; you can see them from our garden if you look. And he sells them to Christians, but with the usury of a Jew."

Now even the old woman teased him, but he did not give up his magisterial dignity.

"Of course I sell them to Christians. There are no enemies of Christ here, even though my clients are in a way."

"In what way?"

"They're all thieves and crooks, and if they can steal a pig from my pen they don't think twice about it."

"It's the same everywhere," Aroldo dared to intervene. But the old man, having looked him up and down, especially in the face and in the eye, decided it was not necessary to honor him with an answer. His attention was ever more fixed on Concezione, in whom he noticed a profound change. But her face of tarnished silver, her eyes, once dark and shiny like onyx, now faded and veiled with sadness, her whole emptied person, awakened in him a sense of ridicule instead of pity.

But only after he had pondered the effect that his words would create, he asked coldly, "What have you done, Maria Concezione? You are all dried out like a tree that has lost its leaves."

"Autumn comes for everyone. For you it's already winter," she answered. Then she assumed a serious air, and Aroldo understood that she spoke more for him than for the old man. "I have been at the hospital because I had a serious illness in my nose. They took a lot of blood from me, I suffered a lot, and I am still not well."

"But your voice is clear," observed the visitor, not without malice. "A friend of mine, who had a worm in his nose, waited for it to come out by itself; but he was left without his voice. And you were wrong to have gone to those crooked doctors. If you had stayed home and sat in the sun, the illness would have gone away by itself."

"Maybe you're right; but I couldn't breathe anymore. I couldn't work anymore."

"Work! As though your father, the blessed Antonio Giuseppe, didn't leave you enough to live on? Ten thousand scudi he left you, besides the house and the church. And you haven't buried them under the altar, no, but like a good girl you have invested them at interest in the bank. And you did the right thing."

Concezione blushed, because Aroldo didn't know she had this capital, just like most of the people in the town didn't know about it.

"It's not at all true," she lied. "I only have a little money, and I have now spent it for the operation and the rest."

Without moving, without even moving a finger, his hands still, one on top of the other, on the cane he had placed across his lap, he replied, "What do you mean, it's not true at all? You're telling that to me? You have a brazen face, my flower. Your father, the blessed Antonio Giuseppe, my Compare of baptism, since he was the godfather to my four grandchildren, had land, woods, and livestock. When he became sick he told me that he needed to sell everything and place the money at interest, since those poor women didn't have anyone to look after the stuff,* and taxes and thieves would take it all away. This means that when the girl comes of age and finds a good husband, she can repurchase the land and livestock. And so it was done. You were ten years old, Maria Concezione, and I'm sure you remember everything perfectly well."

"I don't remember anything," she said discourteously.

Unperturbed, as though Aroldo's presence were a shadow, he continued, "But I said, 'Compare Antonio Giuseppe, two of my grandsons, your godsons, Pietro and Paolo, will be almost grown up when your daughter is old enough to marry.' And he understood, and was happy. But you, Maria Concezione, have never wanted to hear this. You haven't listened to your father's wishes because you seem like a goody-goody but you have a heart of stone, and an even harder head, may a lightning bolt crack it."

---

*La roba. See the discussion of "stuff" in the afterword.

"Compare Felice!" protested the old woman, while Concezione laughed again, gazing into her coffee cup.

"Send your grandsons to a nursemaid if you don't know what to do with them," she said shrugging her shoulders.

"Ah, you want to send them to a nursemaid. I know why, just like I know very well why you laugh at me and everyone else," shot back the old man. Then he was quiet for a moment, and Aroldo was almost afraid of the silence, broken only by the slightly nervous tapping of Concezione's spoon in her empty cup. He listened calmly, asking himself if he shouldn't be going; but he had the impression that the old man was talking to him, to let him know the life, character, and means of Concezione, and possibly to dissuade him from his amorous plans.

And, in fact, Giordano went on, "I'll tell you why. You look like the Virgin's little sister, but your looks deceive, dear daughter, they deceive. In this you resemble your father's ancestors. I say your father's, because your mother's were all made of good stuff; we have proof of that in this little woman, who truly is mother and sister of Most Holy Mary."

"Amen," said Giustina, who, however, didn't seem very flattered. "I would have thought at least that your evil tongue wouldn't have anything to say about my husband."

"Your husband, the blessed Antonio Giuseppe, was my Compare of baptism, and he wouldn't have been if he hadn't been more than honest. He was a banner, your husband, a flag in a procession. But his father, and the father of his father, may all their souls be saved if they aren't already, let's say, in Purgatory, everyone knows what they were like. Beautiful to look at, beautiful as statues, but, but . . . "

This time it was Concezione who protested proudly, "Talk—go ahead and talk. There's no reason why a man like you, who doesn't respect the living, should respect the dead."

"I haven't come to argue," he continued calmly, and the words continued to flow from his satyr's mouth, sonorous and even, like the water from a fountain. "I came to say hello, since I haven't seen you for a long time. But if you really want me to, Maria Concezione, I will remind you that the father of your grandfather was reputed to be part of, indeed, to be the leader of, an expedition of brigands against a rich priest who, may his soul rest in peace, was half a brigand himself, and who had become rich with church money. Among other things, they say that under threat of excommunication or refusal to celebrate marriages, he took the first night with the bride for himself, and did other evil deeds. This unworthy servant of God had built a villa for himself in one of his vineyards, and he was often there making strong wine and spirits with his own hands, and then inviting his buddies to enjoy it all in happy company. It was after one of these little parties, when the friends had left, that a group of masked men attacked the priest's house. Since he refused to tell them where the money was hidden, these good old boys tied him up and set his bare bottom on a tripod over a fire. He had the scar the rest of his life."

"Fairy tales!" said Concezione. "And they tell this business of the tripod in lots of other stories like that."

"Very well, but this is what happened. After the story with the priest, and other smaller capers, your great-grandfather, who had been a poor goatherd, bought land, cows, houses. He died rich, and your grandfather, who followed his father's example more cautiously, it's true, but successfully, became even richer. But the priest's excommunication weighed on your family. The brothers of your grandfather all died bad deaths, and he, after an infection they say came from a wound, lost his right arm, the one with which he had done the evil deeds. Then the devil became a hermit: he built this church and these little rooms for himself and his descendants to live in, and he had masses said every Sunday and the other feast days for the good of his soul. Is this also a fairy tale, Maria Giustina?"

The woman did not reply, but her face was sad, solemn; and Concezione didn't protest any more either. After all, she thought, it's better that Aroldo know these things, he'll resign himself more easily. And she and her mother knew very well that everybody in the village and its surroundings repeated these stories that old Giordano had just told.

He went on, "Compare Antonio Giuseppe, that good soul, obeyed his father. He did good deeds, but he also provided that after his death his widow and daughter would live peacefully, without any cares. He did well; who doesn't approve of him? I am the first to do so; wherever I go I honor his memory. But you, Maria Concezione, why do you want to deny your father's goodness? Why do you pretend to be poor, forced to work, when he left you set like a lady? Are you afraid they'll steal your stuff? Oh, sure, be careful, lest some swindler start hanging around, or some brigand does to you what your ancestor did to the priest."

Aroldo laughed, but with clenched teeth, a laugh that stuck in his throat but made his eyes sparkle. He would have liked to respond to the old man, to defend himself, since he felt attacked by him, but he felt sorry for Concezione, and to avoid any further humiliation to her, he decided to go. But he would return, oh yes, he would return. The words of the rough pigherd did not change his heart. If Concezione was rich, all the better for her. He loved her poor; he also loved her like she now was, sick, dried out, and even like the old man painted her: dishonest and maybe wicked and cruel. Rejected, he would go, especially since he couldn't defend her. He didn't even have the right to defend himself from the wild man's insinuations without provoking him further. But he would return, like returning to a fountain, like returning to church.

"It's late," he said, getting up. "I bid you farewell."

He didn't look at Concezione, but he instinctively straightened himself up and stretched, to seem taller, straighter, more linear to her. Then he found his sack and pulled his visored cap firmly on his head; it made his face look as youthful as a boy's. He raised his hand in parting, and set off. Maria Giustina accompanied him out of the door. The night was humid but warm. The mountains, shiny black, smoked like enormous charcoal pits, and around the moon galloped great transparent yellowish clouds. The garden, all wet like after a rain, also reflected that light.

Aroldo stopped, uncertain: it seemed he wanted to say something. Then he shook his shoulders to adjust his sack, and went off with long steps. The old woman followed the tall figure until he disappeared behind the gate, and sighed. She had the impression that the young man was fleeing, justly offended, and she wanted to express her indignation to the evil old man. But he anticipated her with clear satisfaction.

"When I leave," he said, "you certainly won't accompany me like you did that beanpole. But what did he want from you? He has the eyes of a cat and the smile of a swindler. Yes, I was talking about him when I said those things—I know he hangs around your house and that he is nobody's son."

"We are all children of God, Felis Giordano, and our house is frequented only by honest men."

"Yes, I know. The old friends of Antonio Giuseppe come here, and your lady friends, the devotees of your Madonna, and that little priest, my thrice-holy grandson, and the doctor and the phlebotomist, when they go for a walk. Even people from the road stop here, and you accept them all equally. And then there's this beanpole—he knows what he's after."

Concezione was tired and irritated. She looked at him with eyes reanimated with the light of pride and, to her mother's surprise and pleasure, she said, "That young man is my fiancé."

The old man picked up his cane and beat on the floor.

"Good. I told you so, Maria Concezione. He wants to play the trick on you they played on the priest, to squeeze your money from you."

"Let's stop it," said the mother, and because she was a little bit afraid of the Compare, she tried to be conciliatory. "Don't you realize, Felis, that the girl is teasing you? The young man is good and honest. He comes here because Concezione sews his shirts, like she does for other clients, natives and strangers. But there isn't anything else, nor can there be. Tell me, rather, where you have been all this time. And now I'll give you something to drink, too. It's good wine; I bought it to strengthen Concezione, but she doesn't want it. You drink it, to her health."

She brought him a glass of wine, and he seemed persuaded.

Concezione also calmed down. After all, what did it matter if Aroldo had gone away, maybe never to return? Now everything was finished, with him and with the rest of the world. "You are alone with your destiny, Maria Concezione. Your hand has only to brush your breast to remember that your fate is settled. Even the old man's words can only seem empty, like the sound of the wind in the valley." And so she smiled again, but with a vague and resigned smile, when the old man, finishing his drink, announced the purpose of his visit. Now that Aroldo was gone, from fear that he may have stayed outside to listen, the old man lowered his voice and took on a more natural tone.

"Most of all, it's about this: Marcello the blacksmith wants to sell the land that Antonio Giuseppe sold him before his death. Marcello needs money because his grandsons are studying to be doctors, and also because he wants to add on to his house. Well then, that's his business. Our business is the fact that he wants to sell the land at an excellent price; and, since the deed of purchase from Antonio Giuseppe says that in case of resale, he or his heirs have the right of refusal, I have come to ask you what your intentions are."

Mother and daughter looked at each other, but Concezione seemed to have neither the strength nor the will to reply.

"Our situation hasn't changed since the death of my husband. We are still women alone, Felis, and we don't intend to take on any headaches."

"But your situation could change, even soon. You thought I was joking to propose one of my grandsons for your daughter. But they are not boys anymore, not like this perfect woman here says. They are over twenty-three years old, and they are strong and good at everything. Pietro now works on his own: he has fifty cows, and he manages them like fifty treasures. Paolo is with me; he works day and night without tiring. They are both good, without vices, healthy and brave. And I want Maria Concezione for one of them."

"I want! We need to see if she wants!" said the mother, not knowing whether to be cheered or not.

"One or the other. Choose."

"Right. Like choosing the ripest fruit. But do you know you're rushing things, my brother? We don't even know the two boys very well."

"I repeat: they are two giants, handsome and robust. We are all good folk. You know our life down to the roots; we even have a priest in the family. What family is more honorable and hard working? Even my daughter, the mother of the two lads, works like a slave. She's always baking bread, washing clothes, cooking, sewing, and taking care of the house. Serafino, our priest, wants her to get a maid to help out, but she doesn't want any strange women in the house. Only Maria Concezione could please her."

A bit ironic, but also flattered, the mother turned again to Concezione.

"Well then, what do you say? It's up to you to reply."

"As far as the land is concerned, you've given the right answer; we don't need to discuss it any more. Tell Marcello the blacksmith who is looking for another buyer that we won't raise any opposition. As for the rest, it's all a joke; and I don't want to joke, especially now."

"You are pale, daughter," said the mother. "Go to bed; you've been worn out enough today, and this was not the doctor's advice. Go: I'll keep our old Felis company."

But he didn't want to go away with a fistful of wind.

"Maria Concezione, think it over. You don't even know my boys. Very well, tomorrow is Sunday; I'll make them go to mass in your church, then afterwards I'll bring them over here."

"Go ahead, bring them, like two little dogs," she said, getting up, "I'll be glad to meet them. But then leave me alone."

"Two little dogs? They are two lions; two blooming oaks; and you would be well advised to respect them."

"I respect everyone, but I want to be left in peace. Good night."

Her voice was sweet and tired. The shadow of her eye-lashes fell over her dark-ringed eyes. When she had left, the old man also seemed to grow sad, or at least thoughtful. He picked up the glass he had set on the floor, and lowered his voice even more.

"Yes, your daughter is very worn out; we need to make her better. You should give her meat sauce, eggnog, roasted birds. I'm counting on you, Maria Giustina; the girl must get better. And throw out that stranger. He's not the man for you; he's a ragged little man in spite of his size. If he comes back here and bothers the girl again, I'll put him in his place."

Concezione heard these words, but didn't get irritated. She really was tired, and she only wanted to sleep. But stretched out next to the wall in that great cold bed, she remembered that first she had to pray, for the living and the dead, for everyone, even for that deluded old man who, in a low voice, continued to make plans, one sillier than the other. When he finally left, she could pray better. She felt like she was still in the little bed in the hospital, and she smelled on herself the odor of the alcohol with which they had cleaned her shoulders. A night nurse, a nun dressed in black and violet, with a moonlike face and silent, agile feet like those of a cat, brushed her forehead with her warm hand. It was a pleasant contact, which made Concezione think of the feeling of Aroldo's hand, but at once she shook her head against her pillow to free herself from the memory. And Aroldo disappears; the nun remains, black and violet and white like the night. Concezione pretends to sleep and patiently waits to be alone. And when she is alone, in her rented cell on the ground floor of the hospital, she slips out of bed, wraps herself in the blanket, and flees. Not even she knows why she does this; who knows anything for certain in dreams? First she manages everything easily, quickly: everything is smooth and bright. The road in front of the hospital is paved with slabs of granite and shaded by a line of small trees. Other trees, old and dark, lean over the wall around the garden next to the little garden of the hospital. This wall, green with moss, is not so high that Concezione can't see over it. In fact, she sees the rows of cabbages with their white buds, and in the distance a one-story house with a small porch of rusted iron. The moon shines on the glass of the window, and Concezione shivers, as if that brightness were a will-o'-the-wisp. As a matter of fact, she knows that no one lives there and that they say the house is haunted. Still, she stands and gazes at it, drawn by a fearful fascination, until it seems that a shadow passes behind the glass. Then she takes up her path again, coming out into the road that leads to her house. Other trees arise along the embankments over the valley. The moon flits from branch to branch like a silver bird, but farther along it also runs through a milky sky, preceding and giving light to Concezione, until both stop, as if to say something to each other. And suddenly the fugitive realizes that she has lost her blanket along the way, but she is not cold, even though she is dressed in a light dress of black cloth, the same one she wore as a little girl, when she went to school in the town, with a bookbag made of the same cloth as the dress, both sewn by her mother. A little string closes the bag, which she swings like the acolyte does with a censer in her family church. And then, suddenly, this bronzed boy with eyes so big they seem impossible to open fully jumps out behind her and stops the bag. Fear and joy, even happiness, make her tremble and laugh.

"But I am not laughing," says the boy, "I'm not laughing at all. Do you understand?"

She stops laughing and tightens her mouth to keep from responding, like Aroldo had done that evening while the old man talked. And then there is Aroldo on the path that came out of the valley. He is returning from work with his knapsack on his shoulders. And the boy vanishes, but first he gives a yell that awakens Concezione with a start, cold with anguish. She heard her mother snoring lightly on the other side of the bed, and drew near her to get warm, feeling once again like a little girl, afraid of voices in the night, even seeking protection. But she couldn't get back to sleep, nor could she begin her prayers again. The warmth of her mother's body and even her mother's snoring, to which she was accustomed, gave her a feeling of well-being, of defense. Indeed, she seemed to be able to look within herself, to her memories which were in fact her worst enemies, and to conquer them once and for all, and not think about them again.

She began with her walks home from school when she was eleven years old, and she stopped, climbing up on the wall, to look at the garden of the cabbages and the house with the little iron porch. A little family, poor but quiet, lived there: the gardener, his wife, and a little brown boy with shiny teeth always full of blades of grass like those of a little goat. He was the acolyte who assisted at the masses in the little church; he wanted to become a priest, but then he changed his mind. He often changed jobs, without ever achieving anything. He always strolled about in front of the church, and one day, when Concezione was fourteen, he surprised her alone in the house and would have raped her if her mother hadn't turned up in time, driving him away like a thief and threatening to turn him in to the police. And yet Concezione felt drawn to him by an evil power, or rather by a sensual fascination stronger than her strongest will. In spite of her mother's surveillance, she found ways to meet him. It was an almost ferocious idyll, of young beasts in love, helped by the hidden nooks of the place: rocks, bushes, little walls, tall weeds, ravines, solitude and space.

But Concezione valiantly resisted his caresses, and he, for his part, said, "Your mother doesn't like me because I am poor and unfortunate. But you'll see, I'll find a way to get rich and I will marry you. You'll see."

In fact, one day he appeared dressed in new clothes from head to foot, with beautiful shoes and the little pocket of his vest bulging with coins. And he gave Concezione a gold ring, which was meant to be an engagement ring. But a few days later he was arrested, along with others, for the minting and trade of counterfeit money. Condemned to a number of years in jail, he hanged himself in his prison. This was Maria Concezione's secret and futile remorse.

The mother was the first one up the next morning. It was another gray and severe day; the fog had vanished, the mountains appeared naked, with livid spots of forests, the slopes furrowed with reddish stripes, like whipped backs.

"We're going to have snow," announced the old woman, and to comfort herself she immediately lit the fire and put on water to boil for coffee.

Any minute now the little priest would arrive, hurried, with a scarf around his neck, followed by the acolyte. Even though no bell announced it, many people came from town to hear mass in the little church. Maria Giustina was proud of this, as though the faithful came to pay homage to her. For her part, she had a profound adoration for the young priest Serafino, who sacrificed himself every Sunday to come all the way there, even though he was sickly, and, they said, afflicted with a lung ailment. The coffee was for him; she served it to him in the small sacristy while, behind the altar, the acolyte drained the remnants of wine from the mass. She prepared the little table under the green window of the sacristy, and then went to open the little side door of the church. And there, in the still dawning light of distance, down the rutted road, she saw the black figure of the priest approaching. The way he walked, he looked like he had wings, and, looking at him, she felt a tenderness, a maternal longing. She would have liked to take him in her arms and warm him like a baby. She heard his cough, she saw him clutch his cape around his chest, and rush forward. The crooked, almost hunchbacked acolyte instead dallied to knock a branch against the bushes along the leafy banks of the road.

Unable to do anything else, she flung open the door and greeted the priest with a deep bow, while he made one just like it to the Madonna, and then hurried into the sacristy.

"He's so pale," she thought. "Rather, he's yellow: his hands look like the claws of a bird. While that animal . . . "

The acolyte did not rush; now he knocked the branch against the little wall of the clearing, with a grimace that pulled his mouth almost up to his ear.

"You cursed beetle," said the old woman, "you make that saint wait for you, while he is so good to you."

And she yanked the branch out of his hand, with a desire to try it out on his back. But she didn't do it because a group of little women were approaching, almost all old, with noses red from the cold.

In the sacristy, the priest vested himself without waiting for the acolyte's help. The latter busied himself lighting the candles, and looking in the little cabinet next to the altar to see if the cruet of white wine was there. It was, and he wanted to try it at once, but he was afraid of the old woman who, once the women came in, had left the door ajar and come up towards the altar.

Others of the faithful arrived: old farmers who had frequented the church from the time of their proud youth; also a few young people; also Aroldo. He looked like a gentleman: he wore a gabardine suit with full pockets, and a red and white scarf around his neck made his face seem as fresh and colorful as a rose. He placed himself in the back of the little church, in the corner behind the door, and looked around for Concezione. No, he didn't see her. Maybe she was still in bed; maybe she still felt bad. A tenderness warmed his heart, like the tenderness the women gathered there beneath the altar felt looking at the animated little feet of the Holy Child. He was almost glad that she was unwell, because that was the only way he could explain her hard behavior, her plans for solitude and detachment from the things of the world; but immediately he conquered this instinct which was, basically, selfishness. No, let her be well and strong like before. Let her be happy and good, for herself and for others. "It doesn't matter if she is bad to me; she can trample on me, like you, Madonna, trample on the serpent. I feel I am under your feet, not like the serpent, but like the moon, and I feel happy all the same."

So he prayed, still standing, with his gray felt hat in his hands, looking at his well-shined yellow shoes, and he felt truly content. It was enough to love, and the blood ran hot in his veins, and youth bloomed all around him in the cold little church, with all the roses of hope and of good intentions. But all of a sudden the door was opened brusquely, and almost pushing each other, two young men came in. They made great signs of the cross with holy water, but turning their backs to the altar. Then they sat down on the stone bench along the wall, not far from Aroldo. They looked like twins, rather dark and squat, with great curly brown heads and dark faces with swollen red lips and long thick eyelashes. They resembled the old man Aroldo had left with the women the previous night. They dressed like him too, with short capes and wool gaiters falling over hobnailed shoes greased with tallow.

"They must be the grandsons of that overbearing old man," he thought, growing darker, and he thought he smelled their wild odor. But looking them over well from the corner of his eye, from their oily hair to their thick olive hands with black nails, he thought they were not Concezione's type.

When the priest appeared on the altar, both of the youths threw themselves on their knees, more out of fear of him than out of devotion. Aroldo, still standing, saw them in front of him like a pair of still untamed heifers, and he was reassured. He loomed tall over them, tall as the moon at the feet of the Madonna, and again he was pleased that Concezione had not come, because it seemed to him that even a look from those louts would have offended and profaned her.

But when the mass was over and he went outside with the intention of visiting the women and bringing Concezione the new gift he had in his pocket for her, he was annoyed to see the two brothers, still taking turns pushing one another, maybe as encouragement, were also heading for the little gate of the garden.

So he turned on his heel and started down the path that went down towards the road to the valley. Then he came back up, confused and disoriented, and stood spying next to the garden hedge.

Those two had entered the women's kitchen, without knocking, without asking permission. No one was there, but Giustina's voice was heard in the sacristy; from its half-closed door there came a smell of coffee. One of the brothers carefully crept up to eavesdrop, but came back making signs of comic fear because he had heard Serafino's feeble voice talking with the old woman. Everyone in the Giordano family, including the grandfather, was in awe of the young priest with almost a sacred fear. In the end, he was the absolute patriarch of the family. He spoke little, but everyone in the house knew what they needed to do; and his mother, especially, obeyed him like a docile little girl.

Therefore the two brothers, who had come there at the order of the old man, with the hope that Serafino would have left as soon as the mass was finished, looked each other in the eye; while one gave a malicious wink, the other grimaced with his upper lip and his nose, as though he smelled something bad. They were almost happy that things were going as they were, since neither of them knew Concezione, and they considered her an old maid. Offering themselves in public until she chose one or the other "like choosing the ripest pear" at once humiliated and amused them. Coming to church, along the solitary road, they had given each other quite a few pushes.

"You go first, Judas, you're the prettiest."

"You first, Maccabeus, you're a centimeter taller."

And in chorus they repeated an unmentionable refrain in which a woman expressed the desire to find herself naked between two youths.

And they were happy to get off scot-free with the grandfather who, perhaps to reclaim his control from Serafino, commanded them with blows of his cane, threatening to beat them again if they didn't toe the line. Now he had this idea of marriage with Concezione in his head, and the brothers felt that, if she didn't reject it, escape would be difficult.

They came out of the kitchen, then, determined to slink away, at least this time. In the garden they saw the acolyte, who was still licking his lips from the wine, and who, with his crooked leer seemed to mock them. The older brother beckoned to him with his index finger and said menacingly, "Look here, animal, you be sure to tell our brother that you saw us here. Otherwise we'll put you in a sack like a suckling pig."

And they laughed, remembering that they had often done just that with some little pig stolen, perhaps by common agreement, from their grandfather's pen. Then they were off, happily pushing each other by the shoulders. Behind the hedge, Aroldo had seen and heard everything. For the moment, he felt again a sense of hope, and he waited for the little priest to also leave.

But Serafino lingered in the presence of the women. The old woman said that Concezione had not attended mass because she still didn't feel well, and he asked to see her. The mother went to look for her, and immediately afterwards Concezione, who had in the meantime gotten up, came into the sacristy. Her face was gray and she shivered with the cold, but Serafino could tell with one glance that she pretended to suffer more than she really felt. The mother said, "But go sit by the fire; you'll talk better."

Neither one had a desire for pleasant things, and both, as if by an understanding, shook their heads, remaining standing next to the cupboard where he had replaced his vestments, under the crude green light of the small window on the rocks. The smell of incense, cold and funereal, still came from the door of the little church, and the little cell, with a few old candelabra peeling in a corner, had the climate of a tomb. Serafino was the first to recover from the sadness of these things. He was very slim in his tidy, almost elegant, cassock, his hair a bit curly around his tonsure, like little bushes around a clearing. Like his grandfather and his brothers, he also had a strange, wild air about him, between a bird of prey and a hermit saint; his yellow hands, a bit hooked, contrasted with his large eyes, golden and good. Looking Concezione in the face, he said, "Why didn't you come to mass?"

She hung her head. She would have liked to have told him all about her suffering and the outcome of the operation she had undergone, but she was ashamed. Instead, as if by instinct, she clutched her hands over her breast, as if to hide the emptiness. Nonetheless, with a tenuous, humble voice of confession, she said, "Can't you see I'm sick? I can't stand on my feet. I came out of the hospital yesterday, and I feel extremely weak. Maybe I will never be well again."

"Only the Lord knows about that. Or don't you have faith anymore?"

Then she remembered that he was also sick, with a more certain and incurable illness than hers, and yet he lived and worked like a strong and healthy man, and she felt comforted. A feeling of light came from his words. She lifted her face, looked at him and continued, "The primary physician of the hospital advised me to look after myself, not to wear myself out, not to seek out emotion. Yes, I have faith, and I want to live, both for my mother and to do a bit of good if I can. But I need to be left in peace."

"Is somebody bothering you?"

"Yes. Your grandfather was here last night. I have a great respect for him; he was a friend of my father. But last night he almost scared me. He wants me to marry one of his grandsons, one of your brothers, Serafino. He said he would come back with them this morning to make me choose; and I can't, I really can't."

An ill-contained disdain made the priest blush. Now he knew why his brothers had come to the mass. The old man had left for the sheep meadows at dawn because someone had brought him the news that the night before, while he was lost in gossip in the women's kitchen, twenty pigs had been stolen. Rather than take the two young men to hunt for the thieves, he had preferred to send them to the little church. Concezione's scudi mattered more to him than the pigs!

"I cannot marry," she continued, still and sad. "It isn't pride, it's necessity. I can't marry, not your brothers, nor anyone else; I'll never marry. But I want to be left in peace. Try to convince your grandfather. After all, he wants this marriage he proposes only because he has his eye on that cursed bit of money my father left me."

"It's exactly because your father left it to you that you should not curse it."

"No, Serafino, he knows well, as everybody knows, that money comes from a fountain of faults, maybe of crimes. I would gladly renounce it if it were not for my mother. But she cares about it; and, after all, one has to live. I'm going to die soon, Serafino; but if I should live on after my mother, I promise you I will use that money to redo the church and to give alms. And if I need to, I'll sit at the door and beg."

"Uh, uh," said Serafino, gesturing as if to scare away some ghost, "Let's not exaggerate, Concezione. Your father was an honest and a hard working man; and then, it's not millions that he left you. As far as the rest goes, I repeat, God is great: life, death, our health are in his hands. You need to have faith. Do you know the parable of the boy from Capernaum?"

"I don't remember."

"Very well, I don't have time now, because I need to go to the cathedral for the divine office. But next Sunday, here in this little church, I'll tell everyone that parable, because we are all more or less ill and we all need to heal. As for my grandfather and my brothers, don't worry. They won't bother you anymore, unless . . . "

"Unless what?"

"Unless you like one of them. They are good lads, happy, generous. Very young, it's true, but a good wife should also be her husband's mother."

He was joking, certainly; but seeing the alarm and fear on her face, he also became serious again.

"You know what I should tell you, Maria Concezione? You are a little bit like life. You understand what I mean: everyone looks at life with the hope of receiving pleasure, money, love; but basically life flees from us and gives us nothing but delusions and, often, pain. My grandfather, my brothers, maybe others, look at you because of your fortune, and they think you are a woman who, besides money, can give them happiness. But instead you are a poor creature, weak and unhappy."

She understood. A spectral smile showed her large teeth of shining ivory; and Serafino pursed his lips to not show his own teeth.

Aroldo saw him leave, followed by the acolyte who amused himself by pulling on the edges of his cape. He was also jealous of this little priest, made of nothing and of everything, who had stayed longer than necessary in the house of the two women. He came nearer, but before pushing open the little gate, he stopped once more to look down towards the valley. Everything seemed petrified, even the grass, the bushes, the bare, gray trees. As the day had gone on, the cold had increased; an opaque cold, still, barely broken by the cry of a sparrow. But that flickering of life, and the smoke rising from Concezione's chimney, were enough to sustain the hopes of that solitary stranger. Without trying to hide himself again, he entered the little garden and approached the door. It was closed, but warm from the heat in the house, and from out of the cracks there came the perfume of coffee. He sniffed it like a flower. He wanted to kneel down on the threshold like a pilgrim in front of a closed sanctuary, since that was his sanctuary, his respite, his joy in life. He knocked: once, twice, three times with his frozen knuckles. The women, intent on making their huge bed, did not answer, but the little door answered for them, and seemed to want to open by itself to let him through.

"Patience, Aroldo, today is really a contrary day; but everything can be won with patience, good will, and above all with the power of love." And so, after a few minutes, Concezione in person came to open the door. She opened her eyes wide when she saw him, apparently vexed. But still he saw the spark of joy shining in the black pupil where his lovesick image was reflected, and so he did not yield when, almost blocking his path, she exclaimed, "So early? What do you want?"

He would have liked to respond that there had already been other visits before his, but he contented himself with a smile, as he drew out of his pocket the parcel that had swollen it.

"I was at your mass, Concezione. Today is your saint's day. Take it."

Since she did not take it, but rather pushed back the gift with hostility, he took on the desolate air of a little boy about to cry. And if he didn't really do so, it was because the old woman suddenly appeared, greeted him kindly, and took the parcel.

Everything was welcome in those tight times when the bank had disastrously cut the interest on deposits, and Concezione couldn't work anymore, and when the weather threatened a snowstorm.

"Come in, son, come in. You are always welcome."

He entered cautiously, like a cat in a strange house. He wanted to sit down in the corner behind the door like old Giordano, but the old woman pushed him towards the stove.

"We haven't even finished your suckling pig, and you bring us other stuff, you spendthrift. What do we have here? Ah, cheese, and good cheese, too. Very well, today we'll have a celebration: come eat with us at noon, I'll make you macaroni."

He stood with a bowed head before the stove, hat in hands, in the same posture he had in church. He did not dare to accept, but the invitation itself consoled him. He wanted to crouch in the corner of the stove, to say humbly, "Let me stay here; I won't breathe a word. Keep me here like a faithful dog, at least until I can return to my work. I can't stay in town because my companions visit loose women and then go to the tavern; then they walk through the streets, drunk and happy. I feel lost in their company. I don't drink, I don't sing. My drunkenness and my joy are here."

"Will you come or not?"

He turned his head, looking for Concezione. She had disappeared. Still, he felt freer and he said yes.

All day long the sky hung low, uniform, the air icy and still. It was a dark day that seemed to plan a crime but decide not to carry it out. It decided during the night, in the dark, in the striking silence that helped commit it. But it was an innocent crime, and early in the morning, when the old woman went to open the little door, she found it blocked by a little marble stair of snow, and a moving curtain of white lace. She stood watching, almost as happy as a child, even though the spectacle was not new to her. And she did not completely close the door against the welcome guest (snow is the wool of the fields; with its warmth they happily become fertile). The cat also went out, sniffed, and came back in sneezing.

The fire was soon started; the coffee boiled again; again all of the humble things of the house became cheerful. Concezione also cheered up, in that great, warm bed that smelled of stubble like a mown field. She thought that, at least for one day, her suitors would not come bother her. Still, the memory of Aroldo did not want to leave her: his youthful, healthy figure, his fresh mouth that tasted of neither wine nor tobacco, his eyes, filled with blue, his prudent yet passionate silence, all of this pleased her and awakened her tenderness. And she was sure of him, even if he seemed somewhat intimidated and put out by the news of her wealth. But the shadow of her destiny did not leave her; she felt like a nun who could not and did not want to be free of her vows. If she pushed Aroldo away it was for his own good, for love and nothing else. "Virgin Mary, you who hear all who turn to you with the faith of the blind man sure to see light again in another life, Mary full of grace, hear the prayer of your poor Concezione: take this arrow out of her heart, let her not think of Aroldo with carnal desire any more." She recited the Hail Mary three times; by the third she felt the warmth of divine protection brush her heart. Her mother entered the room; she went up to the half-closed shutter of the window, and, after passing her hand over the misty glass, said, "Goodness! People are traveling even in this weather!"

She saw, in fact, a strange mounted figure approaching on the lonely road. The horse was black; it continually shook its tail and ears to free itself from those innumerable white flies that fell from the sky. Black too was the figure that rode it, all wrapped up in a cloak, with warrior's spurs on tall shoes, the tip of the hood fringed with snow like the top of a mountain.

"Oh," continued the mother, ever more surprised and curious, "now it's stopping right in front here. Is it a man or a woman? Now it's dismounting and leading the horse towards our gate; it seems to be heading this way. Oh, Jesus and Mary, it's her, that devil of a woman Comare Maria Giuseppa."

And she ran into the kitchen to open the door. The woman with the spurs had definitely entered the little garden, pulling her horse after her and vigorously stamping through the snow, cold and granular like flour. In the arc of the hood that was firmly tied under her chin, was a pale, fat face, with a thin mouth topped by a mustache like that of an adolescent boy. Her flashing black eyes looked out like those of a fox from the depths of her lair. The voice was also masculine, and boomed in the silence of that place.

"Greetings, that's all. Greetings, Comare Giustina. Am I welcome or not? My knapsack is full."

"Full or empty, the knapsack is yours. Mine is the pleasure of seeing you again."

At that, the guest stretched out her hand and caressed the face of Comare Giustina. Then, knowing her way around the place, she herself led the horse under the roof that covered the well and sheltered a few chilly chickens. She tied a sack of oats around his neck, pulled off the knapsack and the saddle and carried them into the kitchen, first taking care to shake the snow off herself.

"I allowed myself to stop at your house not for my sake, but for the sake of my horse; otherwise I would have had to take the poor beast all the way to the courthouse. I have an appointment that will last who knows how long, because those judges, may the plague take them, do things at their convenience."

Even though she had bent down to take things out of the knapsack, she made signs of exorcism against the judges, while the other woman, already softened by the presents that the generous guest had brought, gave her many compliments.

"You are always the same, Comare Maria Giuseppa; always bold and brave and young. But why always these lawsuits that won't leave you in peace, not even at the Last Judgement?"

"That day least of all! But it will be the day of true justice, when I will take from Lucifer's hand the pitchfork he uses to poke the damned and use it against my enemies, bare and helpless, may they and all their offspring be damned!"

"What case do you need to discuss today? Couldn't it have been postponed because of the weather? Don't you have a lawyer?"

Without ceasing to pull little baskets and parcels out of the knapsack, the woman raised her ferocious face. "A lawyer? I've had three, who gnawed my bones down to the marrow. At the Last Judgement, they will be the first to be poked with the blazing pitchfork. And I'll bite them, too, because I am so angry at those villains that my teeth will still be good after my death. For the moment, I am the lawyer for my case. I need neither paper nor pen—I have my tongue, and that's enough."

"Calm down, Comare Maria Giuseppa. Have a cup of coffee; it will warm you up and do you good. And tell me the news about your husband."

"My husband is well. Deaf as a stone, blessed as an angel of heaven, he doesn't worry about anything but his pipe. He sits all day in front of the fire, never thinks about the business of the house. No, but I'll tell you about him later. Now I am in a hurry."

Puffing, heated up like on a summer day, she almost spilled on her hostess the cup of coffee she was handed. Then, with a great tug, she put on the table the basket she had pulled out of the knapsack.

"This is for Maria Concezione. What's the girl doing?"

For her, as also for the mother, Concezione was always a girl, and Comare Giustina was touched.

"She isn't very well, she is still in bed. Do you want to see her?"

"Right now I'm in a frenzy. I have to be in court at nine, and it's a distance from here."

And she ran out like a black ghost, the ghost of winter, leaving on the snow footprints full of holes from her hobnailed shoes.

Maria Giustina didn't know whether to laugh or be serious. She loved the shrewish woman, rich and contentious, with whom she had been friends for many years, but she thought her somewhat crazy. She came from a little village on the mountain, a poor group of shepherds' hovels, of which she could consider herself the queen. Her husband was much older than she was and left her free in her extravagances. Without children, mistress of land, herds, a lot of money, she was always in litigation with the owners of adjoining properties. She fought over every small thing: rights of passage, boundary lines of a few centimeters of land, rain water drainage, trees that hung over the little boundary walls. And she stretched out these conflicts until she made of them a continuous, impassioned, vital fight—not out of greed, nor because of pride, nor even out of an instinct of property, but because she needed to agitate herself, to vent the exuberant energy of her robust body and her overbearing nature.

Concezione, still in bed, had heard the incursion of her mother's Comare—they were Comari of Saint John,* because they had first met, as brides on their honeymoons, at a country fair; and, while their respective husbands drank and played *morra*,** they became tied in friendship by exchanging handkerchiefs tied with seven knots. And she was cheered up by the diversion that the guest brought into the small home.

With Maria Giuseppa, there was always entertainment: her stories, her disputes, her superstitions, her noisy and sincere way. And her gifts were extraordinary and refined. She had brought "the girl" unusual things: fresh grapes, pears, almond sweets, and a jar of honey. And to her Comare she brought a whole ham, and dried cheese curds.

---

*St. John's Day, the Feast of the Nativity of St. John the Baptist (June 24) is a traditional time for midsummer revels, including bonfires.
***Morra*, a counting game played with the fingers, is a tradition of Italian tavern life.

"This is really the house of gifts," said Concezione, "but we'll have to pay them back."

"What do you want to pay back to her? She already squanders everything she has, and besides, at her house there is so much stuff she doesn't know what to do with it all. After all, it's our little Madonna who protects us. She's the one who makes these gifts come to us."

Concezione also believed this. On this faith; neither blind nor fanatical, but tranquil and luminous, the flower of hope, she always floated, like a water lily on clear water. Perhaps even her illness was a mysterious gift which had saved her from sin and other sorrows. God's will be done.

And yet Aroldo kept appearing before her, with his eyes, which also looked like flowers of light; and she thought that he might not have been able to return to work that day, and so would have a very sad day.

To free herself from her thoughts, she got up, even though she felt very cold, and said to her mother that they should at least prepare a good meal for their guest. She made a dough of a bit of flour, with egg and lard, and she made from it a lot of little braids that she fried and smeared with honey. She truly felt like she was a girl again. Her mother was also busy. Good smells spread throughout the little house, smells of hospitality and therefore almost of a holiday. Nor was the horse neglected: Giustina watered it, mixed a bit of hay with the oats in the sack, patted its head. It was a good and patient beast. It seemed to be made of varnished black wood, so much so that the overbearing rooster, all yellow and red like a flame, pecked at his hooves as if to see whether they were real or false.

And the snow continued to fall, less thick, but incessant, and light as the hawthorn flower dropping its petals. It was so silent that the chewing of the horse and the imploring peeping of the hens reached the kitchen.

But then, after noon, to once again enliven the place, Comare Maria Giuseppa returned. She also sat in the corner near the door, like old Giordano, with whom there was a hint of resemblance—they were at least from the same people—

saying that she was deathly hot. She threw off her cloak, and appeared in a dress of dark cloth bordered with yellow and green, that clung tightly to her powerful person. Her skirt was so short that one could see, above the little shoes tied with rawhide laces, white stockings with red monograms,* solid legs, a bit bent from riding horseback. After having looked hard at Concezione, shaking her head over seeing her so wasted away, she began to tell the story of her hearing at the courthouse. It seemed that she was making a summary to herself more than to her guests. With high and low voices she imitated the voice of the judge and of the clerk, in such a way that Concezione was as entertained as she had hoped to be.

It had to do with one of her usual cases, a contesting of a hovel that Maria Giuseppa had bought without a formal contract of sale. But it seemed that she was talking about a castle, and it all involved false testimony, insults between the parties, threats of fire and death, and also a hex which the opposing party had set in motion against the new owner of the contested hut.

"Yes, I found in a corner under the arch of the hayloft that I pass under every day a long stick with a little knot of rags all stuck through with pins. Every pin is one misfortune. In fact, I had begun to feel pains in my bones when I made this dis-covery; but I made so many exorcisms and curses that I later found out one of my adversaries was sick with lumbago. He couldn't even come to the hearing today, and it serves him right. The judge himself said that one who does no evil should have no fear of evil."

She certainly put sentences of her own special invention into the mouths of the men of law, and she seemed to act out an ancient tragedy, citing articles of law she knew by heart, like a poem: the penal code, and the civil code, and the com-mercial one too.

---

*Monogrammed underclothing was a mark of wealth in peasant society of early twentieth-century Italy.

The hostesses listened to her with interest as the mother busied herself cooking the pasta and Concezione set the table. All at once, she changed her tone of voice and demanded, "But who is that simpleton I saw walking around the church twice when I came in? He has an umbrella, and he seems to have lost something in the snow."

"He's lost this," said Maria Giustina, tapping her forehead with a finger, and she laughed jovially, looking at Concezione, whose face had darkened: they both understood that it was Aroldo.

"Oh, certainly," said the guest, "only a crazy man could be out like that in this weather. He won't steal my horse, will he?"

And she bounded to the door, to keep an eye on the vagabond. He also had seen her enter the house of the women, and had disappeared.

"Just as well, he's not there any more. At least, unless he's hidden himself. I swear I'm not afraid of anyone, not the living or the dead, but crazy people fill me with an incredible terror."

"He's not crazy, be reassured, Comare Maria Giuseppa. He's a stranger who works on the road that's being built, and today, with this weather, he has the day off. Come to the table."

At the table, she began again to talk about her enemies. This time she had it in for her relatives.

"Your people, your death. They all try to suck out your blood, they all wait for your death so that they can enjoy your stuff. Only my brother Gaspare loved me a little; but the Lord took him when he was still young, the Lord took him like a shepherd to his service. Gaspare left only an illegitimate son, Costante. He's a good lad, in fact, too good, a bit simple, but a worker. He loves me too; in fact, he's the only relative who loves us. And so, I'm going to leave my stuff to him, but he needs to find a good wife. And who is there up at our place? Girls dying of hunger, ragamuffins in tattered skirts, daughters of beggars or whores. My husband and I always intended to adopt a daughter, find her a good husband, leave her our stuff. Until now, our search has been in vain; now I am looking for a good wife for Costante. She will be rich and fortunate, and she will be the boss since the lad is, I repeat, a bit simple and needs help. Do you feel up to it, Maria Concezione?"

First Concezione wanted to laugh; then she turned all at once to her guest, staring at her with almost frightened eyes. Oh, now her too? It was really a persecution. But her mother had caught the ball on the first bounce, and the thought that her daughter might one day become very rich lit up her imagination. Still, she said, "Concezione is poor, and at the moment she has no plans to abandon her old mother. But we thank you for your good intentions, Comare Maria Giuseppa; and we hope that all your wishes will be fulfilled. Now, let's enjoy this hour of relaxation. Eat, eat another piece of pork."

The guest did not have to be urged: the trip, the cold, her fatigue had opened an abyss in her powerful stomach. And she drank as well, since, to make the hospitality complete, there was no lack of wine on the table.

Then she became affectionate, with a cordial humanity that emerged from her shining eyes and, at times, filled them with tears. And she gazed on Concezione's hard face as if on the face of a marble saint from whom she still hoped for a miracle.

"We need you, my rose. Our house is full of every gift of God, but it's as cold as the house of death. We need a heartfelt soul, and children, and hope, and love. My husband seems at peace, with his fire and his pipe, but when he is alone he sighs and sighs. No one says, my rose, that you would have to abandon your mother. She can come live with us—the house is as big as a convent. And if she wants her freedom, I have other houses nearby, and they are all at her disposal. And she can have serving women and serving maids if she wants them, and also a garden ten times bigger than this one. I can even have a church built if she wants one. All you need to do, Maria Concezione, is to lift this melancholy from my soul, to become our daughter."

Concezione listlessly picked a few grapes from the bunch the guest had brought, and did not answer.

"Don't think," continued the temptress, "that I want you in my house so I can take advantage of you. You would be a lady, a queen. You could get up whenever you want, we'll bring your coffee to you in bed, we'll wash your feet, we'll light a fire in your room. You'll have as many maids as the wives of Solomon. In the springtime we'll go to our fields, where the grass is as high as the water of the sea. We'll shear the sheep, have a party, and lie down in the shade of the trees. You know how beautiful it is to listen to the birds in these trees, and the wind rustle through the branches. And a servant will play the accordion. And we'll eat fresh cheese cooked with honey, and sweets made of candied citron. If you want coffee or *rosolio*,* you'll have it right at hand. If you want to, my heart, you will go to all the fairs, even the farthest ones, on horseback or in a cart covered with an awning, or even in a carriage. You'll only need to express a wish and it will immediately be fulfilled. And if you have children, we'll make the bishop come with his miter to baptize them."

Only this prospect touched the hard heart of Concezione; but it was like the wind that, in the words of the guest, rustled through the oaks of the plateau in spring noontimes: the breath of an illusion.

The other went on, "Do you know how much stuff there is at my house? I don't exactly know myself, to tell the truth. Closets full of sheets, tablecloths, and antique cloth; chests completely full of blankets of wool, of cotton, of silk—in fact, I want to give you one so you can see how well they are woven. Good stuff, not like those cobwebs they sell in the shops. And we have a treasury of things of gold and silver: rings with carnelian, and earrings, and necklaces of coral. And a rosary in filigree with gold beads, and a cross in which you can see the true image of Christ. It's a talisman; they say it comes from the Holy Land and that it protects you from a bad death. And then I won't even tell you about the food stocks. Every gift of God is waiting for you: jars full of oil,

---

**Rosolio: a sweet liqueur.

and grain, and flour, and almonds, and beans, and lard, and dried fruit. We even have the fruit of the jujube, and dried olives as big as prunes. When the traveling salesmen come to the village, they unload their stuff at our house. But what good is it if no one enjoys it? My husband only wants soup made of spelt, and I myself like barley bread and baccalà.* We need children to crack the nuts and chew the dried chestnuts, and young people to nourish themselves on roast lamb and pork liver. A house like ours, where there are no people, is like the sacristy of the cemetery, I say: no fire can warm it, no sacks of money can make it happy."

"It's true; it's the pure truth," admitted Maria Giustina, a bit bewitched, also a bit moved to pity by the plaintive tones of the guest. She looked at the unrelenting Concezione with supplicant's eyes. Concezione had finished the bunch of grapes, and nibbled on one of the sweets she had made; those the guest had brought, even though they were covered with sugar and in the vague shapes of little birds and flowers, made her nauseous. The very idea of living in the rich countrywoman's house "full of stuff" made her feel like she was suffocating. And then, when Maria Giuseppa gave a detailed portrait of her nephew Costante—tall and dark, with thick hair and strong like one of those ancient shepherds come from Libya, but a bit of a stutterer, and so simple that he was still afraid of scarecrows and wild cats—she lost patience and said, "A thousand women would take him with their eyes closed, but it's not for me."

"All right then, I understand: you don't want him. Who do you want, then? The king of Spain?"

"I don't want anyone; don't be offended. I am already old. I am sick. I won't marry anyone."

So hope was not completely lost, and Maria Giuseppa continued, undaunted, to list her goods: plots of land surrounded by walls, livestock, horses, hives, forests of cork which produced a good income all by themselves. But Concezione, leaning back a

---

*Spelt: a grain related to wheat. Baccalà: salt-dried codfish.

bit against her chair, half closed her eyes, and waited only for the moment when the guest would leave.

Serafino returned the following Sunday and kept his promise about the sermon. The weather had become milder, so it wasn't very cold in the little church. There were a fair number of people there, all women, aside from a few old men and Aroldo, who was timidly kneeling in the rear corner. From the altar, the priest told a sort of fairy tale that, little by little, engrossed the humble listeners with an almost musical fascination.*

"The house was barely finished: it was beautiful, solid, white, with terraces and verandahs for the hot season, and rooms with carpets and fireplaces for the winter. Many servants had put it in order, and they cultivated the garden full of palms and flowers. It was the ruler's house, that is, the house of the captain who governed the city. And this city was called Capernaum and was in Palestine, at the time of Jesus Christ. The ruler was a pagan. He did not believe in God, and derided the new religion of the Messiah. And so he came to live in the new house with his family: his wife, his mother-in-law, and a young boy who was his whole joy and hope.

"The son was barely twelve years old, but he seemed older; perhaps he had grown too quickly. The grandmother and mother trembled at every breath of wind that could hurt him. In fact, no sooner were they in the new house than he got sick. The grandmother, who was a Hebrew, tried the ancient exorcisms: she took an offering of two doves to the Temple, and never stopped crying and praying. The ruler, who was already pretty overbearing and wicked in peaceful times, became almost ferocious when he saw his son grow ill. He mistreated his soldiers

---

*This sermon is based on John 4:46–54. Other versions of this story, in which the person healed by Jesus is a servant or a slave rather than a son, are told in Matthew 5:8–13 and Luke 7:1–10. See the afterword for a discussion of the role of this sermon in the novel.

and servants, cursed, and became furious over every little thing. Only the mother seemed gloomily resigned. She said, 'I knew it; when the house is finished, in comes death.'

"They called the most famous doctors, but none of them knew how to diagnose the boy's illness. Meanwhile, the poor little thing was slowly being consumed; he always had a fever and he refused food.

"They also called a doctor from the city of Cana, near Jerusalem. As he left, he said to the father, 'I'm sorry, but the boy's illness is one of those for which there is no cure. Not even the Rabbi, with his miraculous claims, could cure him.'

"And it was like a rainbow suddenly appeared in the clouds that had oppressed the captain's heart. The Rabbi, as Jesus was called in those days, went around preaching in the various districts of Palestine. The ruler was charged with keeping an eye on him and his followers; but as I said, he didn't pay much attention. He thought the Rabbi was a fanatic, almost a mad man. But since he had already consulted magicians and witches about his son's illness, he thought he would go in search of the man who, they said, worked miracles, and ask him for some medicine. And just this thought filled him with hope.

"In those days the Rabbi was, in fact, in the city of Cana. And so the captain went there on horseback, with a few servants. He found the whole city in celebration; it looked like springtime. All the windows were full of flowers; songs and music came from the taverns. Many people were headed for one house almost on the edge of the city, and the ruler, leaving his servants and horses in the courtyard of a garrison, also went off to the place where the crowd was rushing. It was almost evening. He saw a large fire burning on the threshing floor in front of the house of a peasant. Jesus was sitting in front of it, in the midst of many ordinary men. He was dressed all in white, and it seemed that his body shone like silver. Even his fingers were like rays, and his hair was the color of just spun silk.

"At least, that's the way the ruler of Capernaum saw him. His appearance, armed and dressed in his captain's uniform, awakened a sense of fear, because everyone thought he had come to persecute the Master and his followers. But Jesus continued to talk, his voice at once sweet and strong, and everyone was reassured. In fact, the captain drew near, serious and sorrowful, with his hands still on the pommel of his sword. When he came in front of Jesus, he said out loud, 'I have a son who is about to die. Rabbi, I beg of you, come down to Capernaum and visit him. But come immediately, or it will be too late.'

"Jesus looked at him, although it seemed that he did not see him, or that he didn't care about him. Nevertheless, he replied, 'Unless you see miracles and signs, you don't believe.'

"The other replied, with desperation, 'Come, Lord, before the boy dies.'

"Then Jesus said, 'Go. Your son is living.'

"The father's heart immediately believed these words, and he went away at once, carrying a great light within himself. He thought he felt burning in his heart the fire in front of which Jesus continued talking with his disciples. And that same night he returned to Capernaum. The servants spurred the horses; they were all full of hope. When they were close to the city, he sent one of his servants ahead to gather news about his son. The man ran; then he returned towards the travelers like a bird of good omen.

'The lad is alive. His fever is gone, he is almost cured!' he shouted with joy.

"The captain, a man who until that day was used to cursing to express his happiness, this time looked up at the stars. It seemed to him that they were crying, but he was the one who was crying.

"Other servants came running out of the house, and the oldest and dearest was also crying.

'The lad has had no fever since the seventh hour,' he said.

"This was exactly the hour in which Jesus had said, 'Go. Your son is living.'

"And the ruler also felt that he had been reborn into a new life, cured of the worst of all ills, the lack of faith. He seemed to be a lad again, like his beloved son, and now to be able to live an eternal youth, since he believed in the word of God. And when they heard his story, his family converted with him."

Concezione was sufficiently intelligent to understand that Serafino was preaching to her. The other faithful listened, it's true, and willingly, and they thought that their sick relatives, and they themselves, could be cured from the most serious illnesses, if Jesus willed it. But they didn't go much beyond this, since they all had faith and didn't feel any need to be converted. Only Aroldo, whose nervous hands tormented his felt hat, understood that the priest was talking about moral salvation as well as physical health; and he accompanied the soft-pedaled music of the parable with his own humble and silent song that filled him with joy and sadness. "Yes, Concezione, you must get better, for your own happiness, for the good of those who live only because of you, and when you are well everyone around you will feel themselves grown young; everyone will be converted."

And yet, in understanding that the priest spoke only for her, he again felt a pang of jealousy. He would have liked to have been in the place of that waxy ghost dressed in lace who appeared at the altar rail as if coming from a supernatural world, and who, with hardly a puff of voice, entered Concezione's heart, while he, with all his ardor and vitality, left her cold and indifferent.

"Virgin Mary, Mary of Solitude, look down on us from your lunar height, and let Concezione and me find each other again in the desert of this life. I am so lonely, and she is lonely too, with her heart that seems bitten by a serpent."

The sense of desolation and jealousy grew in him when the people had left and Serafino lingered in the sacristy. As the acolyte extinguished the candles, the little church again turned gray and cold. What was Aroldo doing in that dark corner, hanging his head like a guilty man? Here was a holiday stretching out in front of him dismally empty and disconsolate. Better to return to the encampment of the road laborers and break rocks to dull his suffering. In fact, he set off, dragging his feet, all the way to the edge of the road, but he didn't have the courage to go on.

The highest cliffs of the mountain, still covered with snow, appeared in the first rays of the sun like blocks of marble; but from the valley came a warm breath, like that of a child asleep. The noise of the stream, swollen with the melting snow, was a lullaby. And that breath rekindled a bit of hope in Aroldo's heart. His keen eyes saw far away, in the shelter of a small cove between the valley and the mountain, the encampment he shared with his companions, made of huts and a few shelters. And he thought about the places he would be going, hopefully, to carve out longer and more difficult roads than this one, and to find his fortune.

"Well, then, it's better that I go. What else can I do here? I'm like the foxes that come up to our camp because they can only find bitter berries to eat, and so they satisfy themselves with the smell of our food. It's better to go. At least "down there" there will be work on a grand scale. I'll make the first bridge; with my first earnings, I'll buy a guitar—I already know how to play it—and on Sunday I'll entertain my companions. And then also, with time, women will come."

He sighed. He thought about whether he had any young relative he could get to accompany him "down there." Not one: he was really all alone in the world.

A crow, then two, then many, flew high across the sea-blue sky; they followed each other with sweet and mournful cries. They seemed to melt in the splendor of the sun.

He thought seriously about the guitar. Before he left with the manager it would already be summer, with hot nights, the red moon over the mountains, the smell of the still yellow stubble. It would be lovely to play the guitar, accompanying himself with the song of the crickets and the flickering of the stars, without words. For certain sorrows cannot be expressed in words.

He remembered that the patron of the tavern in town, where he had gone to eat a few times, had a guitar hanging on the wall. Maybe he could buy it and even take it with him on his trip, and, before leaving, stand in front of Concezione's window one dark night, leaning against the wall with his hat pulled over his eyes, and sing her a farewell serenade.

On Holy Wednesday, Concezione prepared the Sepulchre of Our Lord in the little church. Just a bit under the steps of the altar she spread out an ancient blanket spun and woven by her father's grandmother, the wife of the famous robber, reserved only for use on that sacred feast. It was made of lamb's wool, but it seemed to be of raw silk, with a border of Greek frets in black and asphodel flowers in the background.

In the middle of the blanket, she deposed the wooden crucifix that the rest of the year hung, tired and resigned, on the wall in the corner of the church. When stretched out on the cloth it seemed completely different: the face sweet and olive skinned, full of woodworm holes like one who has suffered from smallpox, free of dust. The body turned upwards, eyes half closed. All the limbs, in spite of being nailed and withered, stretched out, naked and chaste like a branch broken off by wind, truly abandoning rest. Yes, it was like a branch fallen on the grass, broken off by the wind or the pruner: not dead, but ready to sprout again if the earth were to take it back. And Concezione, on that bitter spring day, felt something similar. Seven little bowls, in each of which she had sprouted a bit of wheat in water, were arranged around the head of Christ like a diadem of rebirth. The wheat was white and smelled of starch. It would have worked symbolically, but would have been too melancholy, almost unnatural, like the hair of newborn infants that grows in the dark of the mother's womb, except for the fact that in seven glasses, each one different, the first flowers of the garden and of the embankment above the valley reproduced the colors of the rainbow: violets, daffodils, carnations, white and orange daisies, and periwinkles the color of the March sky. The bouquets were tight and long, and they seemed to smile, childishly, above the pallid tufts of wheat, lighting up the air with their colors.

When she had finished, Concezione kneeled on the open edge of the carpet, bending over to kiss the feet of Our Lord. It seemed to her that the cold of those tired toes was not the cold of death, but the cold of a poor man who has no fire and waits for the first spring sun to warm himself.

And she thought about Aroldo. He too, poor man, he too was waiting for a ray of love. Compassion and tenderness for the dead Christ melted together in her. Even though Aroldo hadn't shown himself again, and she thought she was glad he hadn't, deep down, she felt that their story should not end this way. His image remained in her heart, never growing still, like one who is drowning, but, with all the strength of life, continually coming up to float and save himself. She neither offered him a hand nor pushed him away.

"I haven't sinned," she said to the Christ who died for the love of men. "I don't break your law, so, O Lord, let me love without hope. May I alone suffer for him."

Sometimes, in those first days of spring, she felt herself go down to the depths: "If you can't help me live," the other one said to her, "come and die with me."

And then, while she was still bent over on the rug, the half-closed door opened and a beam of light reached her. The quick, silent figure of Serafino crossed that luminous path, and before she could get up, brushed her head with his hand.

"Well done. You have done it just right."

His voice was also lighter, rosy, if a yellowish rosy; he also seemed to be on the road to healing. It cheered her up, and she invited him to come have a cup of coffee.

They didn't go out through the sacristy; rather, Serafino wanted to walk through the clearing in front of the little church where the hawthorn flowered under the little wall. Then he turned into the little garden, between the beans and the peas, already sprinkled with white butterflies and black with flowers. With peals of laughter like a child let free, he bent down to look at the blades of grass, the moss that covered the stones, the little lizards scampering away.

"If he is happy, why shouldn't I be?" thought Concezione. And all at once she felt truly happy: happy about the beautiful day, the mountains turning green again, the already hot sun. Going to get the coffee tray, she said, "My mother is out. She's gone down to the stream to wash clothes. Did you have something to tell her?"

No, he had come for her. They sat on the stone bench next to the door and petted the cat that tried to jump in their laps.

"Maria Concezione, I have come for you. Has it been a long time since you have seen Aroldi?"

She blushed, but answered truthfully: it had been almost three months since she had seen the young man. And, in calculating that time, made long by the sadness of those hard days, she asked herself how she had managed to live this way, with nothing, like a poor, old, resigned woman.

"Why?" she asked with faint curiosity, immediately worried about Serafino's interest.

"Listen, Concezione, you have to talk to me sincerely. Have you really decided to have nothing more to do with him? Have you forgotten him?"

"Well, I don't really know myself. You can't control your own thoughts. Anyway, it would be better if that young man were to forget about me. I will be glad when the work on the road is finished and he has gone."

"One more thing before I go on with this subject—but don't be annoyed. At your request, I asked my brothers and my grandfather not to bother you. But my grandfather is set on the idea of a possible marriage between you and Pietro. He decided on Pietro," he added, smiling, "because he is the older one. And he has bothered me about it so much that I have also come about that. Is there really no hope?"

"Is this really a proposal of marriage?"

"And why not, if it pleases you?"

Without answering, she took the tray back into the kitchen. Then she returned, sent away the bothersome cat, and sat down rigidly beside Serafino.

"You are in a joking mood today; that means you are well, and I am really glad about that. But let's not talk any more about your grandfather's ideas. You yourself promised me, remember?"

"But you, too, are well now, Concezione: you look like another person. May God keep you to extreme old age. So now there is no reason why you should not think about your own good. As both your friend and your mother's, as a man and as a priest, I don't want your life to go on like this, sad to you, useless to others. It's my duty to give good counsel to the souls around me; and you are one of my favorites, because I understand that you deserve a better lot than the one your imagination wants to make for you. A woman is made to marry, to create a family for herself, to complete the cycle like our mothers and grandmothers have completed it."

"Oh be quiet," she said, trying to take the thing lightly, "I should get married at all costs, then, to someone I don't love?"

"That's not true. I know that you don't want to hear about my brothers. If I brought them up it was to satisfy my grandfather and put his heart at rest. After all, his fixation is harmless, and neither he nor my brothers can hold a grudge against you. But you are not at peace, Concezione. I know you, and you, more than other women, need love. Why do you want to waste your life? Life is a gift of God; you should accept it joyfully."

She hung her head. She understood that Serafino was convinced of what he was saying. In the circle where he was a minor apostle, he wanted the good for the souls living near him: it was his mission. And once again she wanted to tell him about her pain, her fears, but she only managed to repeat, "I am sick, Serafino; I am very sick. For this reason and for this reason only, I want to be free. If this is the only thing that satisfies me, if my life can still be useful to my mother, why do you try to convince me otherwise?"

"But, listen, do you think about the harm you can do, even without wanting to, to those who love you?"

She remembered, and the thought that Aroldo might even commit some foolishness because of her made her raise her face almost in fear.

"Listen to me carefully, Concezione. There is a woman in our village who public opinion says is your father's daughter. Your father was a good man, but ignorant and of little true religion, like most uneducated men when left to their own devices. He had this daughter with a servant, and he didn't care about her. What well-off peasant hasn't had relations with loose women and left a few bastards scattered around the world? Besides, the mother of this girl had relations with other men, so she didn't look after her rights either. The girl grew up under the bad influence of the mother; when her mother died, she followed her path. Now she lives in a little house half hidden in the midst of a garden that looks like a nest of peace and virtue, but instead it's a den of serpents. I have tried a few times to set the woman on the right path, but to no avail. She is content with her evil lot; like all her type, she is unbalanced and irresponsible. I don't despair of calling her back to herself, in time; but in the meantime, I can't do anything. The powers of the devil are too great."

"I know," said Concezione, mortified and pained. "It's a story that has humiliated me and my mother for a long time. I know, and what's more, neither when my father was alive nor after his death could we do anything to make some atonement for his sin. I have often thought about giving at least a part of his inheritance to the unfortunate woman. We know she has no need of material help, and she once refused my offer. She has a wicked soul, and she said she hoped to see us reduced to misery, to see our church destroyed, and to one day be able to help us out with her cursed money. So now the best thing for us is to leave her in peace and pray for her. But now that you are talking to me about her, Serafino, if I can now do anything for her, here I am, ready to do it."

"Look," he replied, a bit disturbed, "what I have to tell you is not pleasant, and before mentioning it to you I wanted to be sure. Aroldi goes often to the house of Pasqua, that is, of that woman. Why does he do it? Out of desperation, or to spite you? Pasqua is beautiful. She resembles you; even though she is older than you, she seems younger, because she doesn't work too hard. She lives a comfortable life, and she knows how to select well among the men who seek her out: she likes them healthy, young, and rich."

"Aroldo isn't rich," Concezione shot back; then immediately regretted it and regained her dark rigidity.

"He's not rich, but he could become rich, at least that's what he goes around saying to anyone who wants to listen to him. And now he chats with everyone. He's become a different person. On all the holidays, he's at the tavern; he plays and he sings and, unfortunately, he drinks. It certainly seems like, as superstitious people say, he's been bewitched. The wicked Pasqua herself is famous for these things, but, certainly, Aroldi got his incantation from you."

"Oh, Serafino," said Concezione, in a bitter reproach, "you shouldn't talk like that. Anyway, what can I do about it? I'm sorry that he goes to that woman; but, believe me, I'm not jealous, and I am not to blame. All men do the same thing. And anyway, one day he will have to leave, and everything will be over."

"I don't know. I don't think everything will be over so soon. Pasqua will ruin him. Maybe she'll get him to marry her."

"So let them get married. Wouldn't that be one way for the unhappy woman to reform herself?"

"You don't understand me, my sister; you don't want to understand me. The man is desperate, he is debauched. No good can come out of this adventure, no matter how it turns out. Only you can and must save him."

"A little while ago you asked me to help Pasqua. Wouldn't one way be to let her future and Aroldo's come together?"

Serafino shook his head and said, a bit irritated, "You talk without conviction. You pretend with me like you want to pretend with yourself. That way we will never understand each other. Life shouldn't be a comedy, Concezione, at least not among people of faith and judgment, as I hold you to be. Now, I am telling you, I have come to put you on notice. You don't play games with the souls of those you love; and you love that man."

For the second time, she blushed. She was about to answer when she saw the half-closed gate swing open, and, sure enough, a woman with a hamper on her head was approaching down the little path. She was from the village of Comare Maria Giuseppa. She also had hobnailed shoes, a strong, hard body like a column, a red and shiny face, and malicious black eyes that laughed with irony to see Concezione and the priest sitting side by side on the little bench, almost as close as two lovers.

"Good day and good health," she said, placing the hamper at Concezione's feet and lifting the cloth that covered it. "Maria Giuseppa Alivia sends you this. It's an Easter present. She would have come herself, but she hurt her foot when she fell off a ladder while she was cleaning for Holy Week."

Once again rigid and hostile, Concezione stood and looked at the things in the hamper, beside which the woman was bent in adoration.

"You see how many gifts of God? Butter, cheese, eggs, pizzas, and salami; solid stuff, my daughter. And, since I came on the horse of Saint Francis,* I can tell you, my daughter, that my neck still feels the weight of that hamper."

Serafino asked, "Why didn't Comare Maria Giuseppa give you one of her horses?"

The woman gave him a dirty look. She was not convinced that a visit from a young priest, at that hour, to a beautiful young woman like Concezione, could be totally innocent.

"I like to walk with the horse of Saint Francis." she said. "To each his own."

"But this stuff is too much for me," Concezione protested. "You could open a store."

---

*"The horse of Saint Francis": on foot.

"Or give a dinner for the poor," the priest added, seriously.

"And then, how will I pay her back? I really don't have anything I could send to Comare Maria Giuseppa."

"You know very well how you can reciprocate," said the woman, looking her up and down with a nod of understanding. "You only need to send your greeting."

Oppressed, but determined to rebel, Concezione turned to Serafino.

"It hardly seems possible, but Maria Giuseppa Alivia also wants to give me a husband. What's so beautiful about me that I am so much in demand? No, good woman, I cannot send your mistress the greeting she wants. I wish her a happy Easter. I wish her every good thing, to her and her family. But she should no longer think about me as anything but a good friend. And this stuff: yes, I will accept it, since it would be discourteous to refuse it, but I will divide it among the poor, as our Lord Jesus commands. He's there inside the church, stretched out on the floor, poorer than all the poor. Would you like to see him, Signora?"

The woman fell to her knees. "You talk like a golden book," she said, turning sad and almost severe. "There are also many poor, hungry people up there where we are. I will take your words back to Maria Giuseppa, be reassured, my soul. And now let me see the dead Christ."

And before leaving, Serafino said, "Concezione, I will send you a few poor mothers with families, and a few needy ones who don't want to show that they are; and you will divide this gift of God among them."

It was like a ray of sun in a day that was, if calm and warm, nevertheless gray and uniform. That Holy Thursday was gray and warm, but still and heavy. The trees were covered with green feathers, the mountains tiger-striped and melancholy like drowsy wild beasts. But suddenly the heavens opened; out flashed a sword of light, touching the pearl-covered almond tree in the garden. And the mountains cast off, once and for all, their winter pelts.

A small man of an indefinable age and station, still slim in his black overcoat cut in the old way, but smart and clean, with a shiny bowler hat on his small and restless head like that of a bird, with gloves, a cane, and patent leather shoes, entered the little church. He bowed without kneeling towards the Holy Sepulchre; but it seemed he did it more than anything else to examine the carpet, one edge of which he adjusted with the point of his cane, and to smell the flowers. Then he went to the house of the women. There too, he looked around well, gave a light sniff, and said in a slightly shaky voice, "Father Serafino gave me the task of telling you that he cannot come today because he is busy with the ceremonies in the cathedral. I happened to run into him in the piazza, and knowing that I was going to take a stroll in these parts, he asked me to stop in at your house. So I have also visited your graceful sepulchre; the word 'graceful' doesn't seem right, by the way, but imagining that our lovely Concezione put it together, I couldn't find a more apt one. Well done, well done; you have taste, young lady. And, by the way, how is your health? It's been awhile since I last saw you."

"It's true; you haven't been around here much, Doctor. But you must have had a lot to do: many ailments come in the winter."

If it hadn't been the good Giustina who said these things, the man would have smiled suspiciously; for he was an old phlebotomist, a bloodletter who had, it's true, practiced medicine illegally, but had lost all prestige after the opening of the hospital and the new theories about bloodletting. And now, half an alcoholic and without one client left, he lived in complete misery.

Remembering Serafino's words, "I will send you some poor needy one who is ashamed that he is," Concezione understood immediately what this was about.

The gaunt but clean face of the man, his sunken and pale blue eyes, the bitter fold of his gray lips, even the suit that recalled his former dignity, awakened in her a profound pity. Without knowing why, she thought of Aroldo as an old man; of Aroldo worn out by a life of work, of mistakes, of vices, those vices which, once they take hold of a man, rot him to the bone. And the restlessness that had gnawed at her in the previous days gave way to tenderness and charity.

"Listen," she said, knowing that she was giving a double alms, "you are just the person I need. I was thinking about you just yesterday. Maybe you know that I was in the hospital for twenty days, for an operation. I won't talk about that because, thank God, everything went well. But I've been left with a great weakness, and I don't know how to cure it. I don't want to return to the hospital, not at all. I still hate it. But you could order something for me, Doctor. If you don't want me to pay you for the visit, I'll make you a little gift."

"Nothing, nothing, he said proudly, tapping his cane on the stones of the fireplace. "Let me feel your pulse."

The pulse beat regularly. Her appearance was fairly good. He looked into her eyes, and a spark was lit in his.

"You know what you have, Maria Concezione? You have the urgent need of a husband."

She laughed, and drew back the hand that he was palpating with his nervous fingers.

"And where will I find this husband?"

"Rascal, daughter of rascals! Where will you find him? Wherever your siren's eyes happen to fall. If you want, I'll send you one, within an hour at the most, at a full gallop."

"Don't disturb yourself, doctor. In the meantime, let's have some coffee, to the health of this future husband."

The man never accepted anything, out of fear that he would be taking alms; but Concezione's way was so graceful that he accepted not only a big cup of coffee, but also the cookies that she offered him. Then Giustina said, "At one time, Doctor, I used to send you an Easter gift, do you remember? My husband always had such a friendship with you, and you were the one who took care of him. Later on, times became hard for us women alone, and I have neglected my duties. But now it seems that things are going better. So, will you allow me, since I can no longer make the trip all the way to your house, and since this wild girl never goes out of her lair, will you allow me to give you a gift? Poor people's stuff, but you will accept the good intention."

"Nothing, nothing," he again protested. But Concezione had run back into the bedroom, and wrapped up some things. She also put in a loaf of bread, one of those which they used to give to friends and to the poor for Easter, as a symbol of Communion like the consecrated host. And she insisted so much that the doctor accepted it.

"Give it here, daughter of thieves."

"Poor people's stuff," repeated the mother.

"Yes, I know. I'm poor, and old, and alone. But one day that old whore, death, will come to set me free."

And he left, angry. But the sparks in his eyes were extinguished by a veil of tears.

Then another impoverished woman came. They called her Madama Peperona,* perhaps because of the big red nose that revealed the same vice as the doctor's. She had a shawl of ancient grandeur, that now looked like a cobweb, and a plumed hat on top of a crown of gray hair, and she also had gloves, with her fingers sticking out of the holes. First, with a certain dignity, she entered the church, shuffling her ragged shoes. She kneeled down in front of the Christ, who lay among the flowers and the grain like a sleeping shepherd, and prayed for a long time. She also wanted to preserve a certain composure, so much so that it was Giustina who went to call her, begging her to accept a cup of coffee.

The woman went into the kitchen and sat down in front of the fire, as if tired from a strenuous journey, the journey of

---

*Madama Peperona: Madame Pepper, that is, chilli pepper.

her disastrous life. She didn't make them insist, but nor did she show greed. Taking off her shreds of glove with a slow, ladylike gesture, she took the cup of coffee and milk, the cookies, the package that Concezione offered her. And Concezione's offerings were not without a motive, since the woman lived in a little ground-floor room, really just a hole, in the courtyard facing the house where, also on the ground floor, Aroldo lived, in a little room he rented from an old peasant woman. Concezione first asked news about this old woman.

"She's sick," said Madama Peperona. "For two months she's had a dry pleurisy. I don't know if she'll survive it. And she's alone, and I can give her little help."

"But what does the doctor say?"

"What doctor? Who could pay one these days? The unfortunate woman is poorer than I am. You could say she lives on what the stranger gives her. But he's good, and when he comes back from work he always buys her something, some medicine; but he's poor too. That's how we poor people help one another, like wounded birds help each other; and God sees everything."

Concezione was glad to have gotten news about Aroldo this way, indirectly, and to know that he was still good. She would have pursued the subject, had not another woman turned up. This woman was truly poor, with a haggard face and the eyes of a hungry cat. This unhappy woman, who had a sick husband and a bunch of children who were also more or less sick, came to see the women every now and then, knowing that she would get some small alms from them. And now she was not sent by Serafino, but pushed by her own hunger and that of her family. Upon seeing Madama Peperona, who in her frayed shawl still maintained an air of dignity, she gazed at her in fear, the fear of having arrived too late. Madama Peperona shifted towards the corner of the stove to make room for her, almost as though she were the hostess. And she wanted to give her the remnants of her coffee, but Giustina was ready to prepare another cup of hot milk, and so the poor woman was consoled. She went away almost happy because of the package that Concezione had silently given her, but also because of that warmth of neighborly love that even her companion in misery had shown.

"To be able to do good," thought Concezione, filled with a sense of joy she had never felt so deeply. This was the ray of sun that broke the desolation of her heart and her flesh, the alms that were given even to her from the heights of heaven.

Until Easter day, the weather stayed sad, almost as if participating in the sorrowful passion of the ever renewed Mystery. There were rare appearances of the sun, it's true, but followed by rain showers and hail. Everything wept, accompanying the weeping of the Mother of God. But on Easter morning, the weather cleared up. The faithful hastened to the little church, and the women took Communion. Even Serafino looked happy, almost radiant.

Later, as her mother prepared the traditional ravioli of fresh cheese and wild mint, Concezione heated a small cauldron of water to bathe herself. She needed a bit of personal cleanliness, to give her body its own part of freshness and renewal.

While the water heated, Concezione, in front of the small window of the room, let down her hair, divided it, and tossed it over her face and chest like a black curtain. With a large comb, with a small-toothed comb, with an old clothing brush, she let fall a snow shower of dandruff. Then she tossed her hair back and repeated the business until her scalp was red. Finally she rubbed her scalp with a wet, soapy handkerchief. It was a primitive process, but it left her hair as fresh and fluffy as if it had been dressed by a skilled hairdresser.

When she had brought the small cauldron into the room, she locked the door. Now it was time for her ablutions, for which five liters of water seemed perhaps too much. Slowly, in order, she laid out her clothes on the side of the bed: the woolen vest, the cotton blouse with blue and white checks, and then the cloth undervest with a bit of lace at the collar, the knitted woolen slip, and finally her undershirt, as long and wide as divine mercy. And she stood totally naked, brown but shining, with her missing breast. She looked like an Amazon of gilded bronze.

With the quick agility of an Amazon, she bent and straightened herself, using a soapy cloth to rub her long, thin legs, her small knees, on which appeared a bit of red like on a just ripening pomegranate, her flat, almost concave, stomach, and under her armpits, smooth as those of a little girl. Finally, to wash her back, she threw the cloth over her shoulder; and up and down, up and down, from the shoulder blade to the opposite armpit, she finished her bath. Nor did she spare the towel, so that it left a few red stripes on the beautiful back and shivering sides. They were pleasant shivers, followed by such a flush of heat that she would have liked to remain naked, her hair down and wet as if with dew. She felt she had become once more the girl who had run to her rendezvous behind the banks of little white daisies. In spite of the mutilated breast and the memory of the warnings of the doctor at the hospital, Serafino's words and counsels gave her a flush of joy. To live—she wanted to live, to love, to forget her sorrows and her scruples. Aroldo's eyes smiled at her through the blue of the little window, and the idea of calling him back no longer seemed so unnatural.

Later in the day, as if to encourage her in this idea, a work friend of the young man came by. Concezione already knew him because she had also made some clothing for him. He was a little old man, but his face looked like that of a boy. He had already had a few glasses of *acquavita* and was in the mood to laugh and chat. He made fun of Aroldo, but it seemed to Concezione that he had been sent by his companion.

"Now he's taken up music; every night he sings like a cricket. It would be pleasant to listen to him if you didn't know that he has crickets in his head—and we know for whom," he added, squinting his green eyes at Concezione. "But he's a good lad, and I would advise you, Signorina, to not be so cruel to him."

"Isn't there someone else you could advise?"

"Yes, there might be. There is a woman who might console Aroldo, in a way to make him put down his guitar right away—everyone knows about her, too. But she's not the woman for him, and I would be sorry if the lad let her ensnare him."

"I would be sorry too," said Giustina, to whom Concezione had not reported Serafino's words. "May I ask who it is?"

And when she found out, she grew red and thoughtful.

"Concezione," she said, when the man had left, "this is a bad business. That woman certainly is doing it out of revenge. We need to save the lad, to save his soul."

Concezione had her pride, she did not want to go herself in search of Aroldo, especially now that this sad adventure was in the way. So she waited for him to return of his own free will. This would also be a proof that he had not changed.

By this time, the road construction was nearing the last slope of the valley towards the town. They carved out the side of the mountain, and the rumbling of explosives was heard all the way up to the house of the women. Now, in the intervals of silence, throbbed the cuckoo's song; it seemed to complain about being disturbed in its solitude. Concezione also complained, in her inner self, restless and uncertain. At other times, the song of the cuckoo had accompanied her resigned silence, her memories of the past, her hope for a life always like this, the same, but peaceful. Aroldo did not come back, and the thought that he went to "that woman" to drink, as if at the tavern, the poison of oblivion, pierced her heart.

Seated on the little stone bench, sewing, she heard the echo of the explosives, the song of the cuckoo, and started at every rustle of footsteps behind the bushes. But she didn't know what she really wanted. The thought of her bleak future did not abandon her, and her waiting was made up in part of superstitious fatalism. She knew she had to trust in God and not feel rancor towards "that woman"; if Aroldo preferred her, it was a sign of how God wanted things. After all, she was her sister, and maybe it was actually part of the divine plan that the legitimate daughter must in some way pay for the sin of her father. Deep down, she wasn't jealous because she was sure of Aroldo's love. He would return, and one sign from her would be enough to have him back again. But sometimes, when she was alone at home and the hours passed slowly, she left the little bench and went as far as the garden wall. The whole valley was now full of life and the faint smells of vegetation. You could see the water of the stream slither from stone to stone like a greenish silver snake, and the song of the finch accompanied its voice. The mountains, too, were reclothing themselves, but without haste. The oaks let fall their old leaves of copper, as if burned by the cold flame of winter, and at the same time showed their new, pearly green buds. Concezione raised her eyes to the blue above the mountain tops, and thought about that other blue.

Everything in the garden was also fresh and alive: the peas climbed all the way up the stakes, the carnations turned red as splashes of blood. Concezione picked a white daisy edged with pink, with a golden eye in the midst of eyelashes of petals, and carried it with her for company in her solitude. But the little flower immediately grew sad and closed, fell asleep, and she regretted picking it so senselessly. Is it possible that one can't live without hurting innocent things?

What about the rumblings of those explosives that seemed to run into and lose themselves among the gorges of the mountain, and then erupt violently through the paths in the thickets, to reach all the way to her, twisting, and finally settling quietly at her feet like menacing and breathless messengers? She wanted to get up, to save herself, as though something truly alive and tangible rolled at her feet; and then, in the intervals, the cry of the cuckoo capped her restlessness. Everything seemed to turn back to her, to remind her that her life was not right, that she had always taken the wrong path and had done wrong, perhaps more so than that other sister, the outlaw. And, if the cuckoo's lament came from another world, the roar of the explosives told her about a subterranean passage that Aroldo dug all by himself to come once again all the way to her, but broken off, like the daisy.

And then one day old Giordano arrived, with a face as dark as an executioner's. He had stored up a lot of indignation in all that time, and he came, notwithstanding Serafino's injunction, to toss it back at the women. He wanted to be received inside, since the open air is only for chatter that gets lost in the breeze. Seated at his usual place, grasping his cane, he began without a preamble, "And so, your beanpole, your tow-headed Jesus, goes to the Magdalene. But you're all in the same family. Of course."

Concezione felt herself pierced like she pierced cloth with a needle, from one side to the other. She saw her mother blush, and then approach the old man furiously, and she was almost afraid she would come to blows with him.

"I forbid you to blaspheme in my house," said Maria Giustina, bending over menacingly. "If you have come to visit, you are welcome, but don't talk like that. What does it matter to you, and what does it matter to us, if a man who is not a relative of ours goes where he likes and pleases?"

"Ah, it doesn't matter to you? It matters to me, though, because of the honor of the town."

"Oh, oh," Concezione allowed herself to snicker, but the old man was seriously indignant this time, and raised his voice.

"You shouldn't laugh, you know, my heart. There's little to laugh about, and you will realize it soon. It matters to me, indeed, because our town is not inhabited only by asses, but also by Christians and gentlemen and level heads. And what have these spineless foreigners come here to do? To bring scandal and turmoil. They are always drunk and they sing like hoarse roosters. What have they come to do? Make a road? But we don't need this road; let the devil walk on it. We know how to walk from stone to stone, like the giants, and to go into flowing water up to our necks. That bridge they're making over that thread of water I cross with one step—it makes me laugh. And I'm talking about myself—I'm an old man—while my grandsons run ahead of the stags, and when they jump that little stream, it wags its tail like their dogs. We are a breed of strong men, and we don't strum the guitar. And if we go once in a while to a woman 'like her' we spit when we leave her lair, and, by my faith, the next day we go to confession."

"And, I repeat, what does it matter to me?" threw back Concezione. But then she was sorry she had; she shook out the piece she had in her hand and went back to sewing, determined not to speak again. She understood that the old man was letting out his anger, so she had to let him finish. But he wouldn't have finished so soon had Maria Giustina, going to the door, not seen the old man's grandsons crouching behind the garden hedge. Now one, now the other stretched his neck to spy inside the clearing, and, as usual, they had to punch each other to stop their grimaces and silly faces. Rather than the two noble stags their grandfather had bragged about, they looked like two little rabbits.

Realizing that they had been discovered, they hid themselves completely. She heard their smothered laughter, and the old woman also began to enjoy herself. She decided to humiliate Giordano by telling him that the stags were there, playing games in hiding. But he seemed to have an arrangement with them, since he knit his bristly eyebrows and came to the door and called them with a whistle, almost like calling a dog.

The two came running, one after the other. Pietro was chuckling, and Paolo timidly let himself be towed along by him. They presented themselves at the door, even the younger one trying to strike a mocking pose, more than anything to make fun of their grandfather and their grotesque situation.

Grotesque, yes, and ridiculous; but still Concezione felt a cold fear, almost a terror, to see the house invaded by those wild men. For the first time, she felt weakness and desolation. She and her mother had no one to defend them and help them in case of danger. And those two scatterbrains who presented themselves with neither dignity nor pride, incited by the over-bearing old man like in a circus game, awakened in her more than ever feelings of contempt and repugnance. Nevertheless, she remained immobile, with her needle unmoving in the cloth, like an image in a painting. She seemed to offer herself to the gaze of the two brothers like the thief who raises his hands to be robbed better. But she was wrong. A veil of submission, if not of admiration, wound itself around the two young men; and only after Giustina had asked them to sit down, reassured by the silence of both women, by their forced but not hostile welcome, did the older one manage to be free and easy, even awkwardly humorous. He turned from one side of the chair to the other, stretched out his legs, and tapped his chest with his fingertip.

"A fearless soldier," he said, "a gorilla, eighty-centimeter chest, healthy stomach, and an appetite to match his courage."

Motionless on his cane, like the old bear admiring the little bear cubs, the grandfather had a happier face. He was hoping.

In fact, Concezione, reassured, took up the light tone of the young man's joking, and, running her laughing glance over his body, said, "Yes, but how did they accept you, with those short legs?"

The other brother broke out laughing in such a way that a sprinkling of saliva scattered on his face; he dried it with the back of his hand. Pietro felt somewhat undermined, since Concezione immediately ran her eyes over the figure of his brother. He knitted together eyebrows that looked like they had been drawn with coal, and rebutted with a seriously men-acing voice, "All right then, I challenge you to run with me, you with legs like a smooth poplar. Try it. Let's go outside and run anywhere you want. I'll overtake you in a flash, even if you have a kilometer's head start. I'll catch you, put you on my shoulders like a mad sheep, and I'll carry you in a run up to the top of the mountain."

His brother gave him a strong thump on the back, either of approval or reproach. He turned to him and said, "Hey, let me be, you son of a crow."

"My mother is your mother, you rascal!"

These were the compliments the two brothers knew how to give one another, as their grandfather continued to look at them, hardly knowing which of the two was more clever. Giustina, though completely reassured, was more severe. She sat with her hands on her belly, like an idol.

"You don't even respect your own mother, wicked boys that you are. Anyway, Concezione will give you some coffee now. I don't have any wine. That little devil Biblino, the acolyte, even drank the wine for mass."

"Wouldn't that have been our brother Serafino?" said the two suitors with one voice, and they began to also make fun of their household saint, now that he was far away and couldn't hear them. "Because he only likes white wine; that's why he's that color and doesn't even look like he's related to our grandfather."

And they laughed at the old man, to show Concezione that they weren't afraid even of him. And they had quite a few other proofs of their courage and strength to show her: for example, how to kill an enemy, in peace or in war, by crushing his head with their knees; or how to stop an angry bull by his horns; or to hunt an eagle, more dangerous than a bull; or how to put out a fire already burning well by beating it with branches. They couldn't demonstrate their skill right then and there, but Pietro, elated by his bragging, dared to look at Concezione's body with the eyes of a male, and a male who knows. And the other one, noticing this, while he himself was afraid to look at her breast, began to be jealous, just like that, only because of a spirit of competition. And suddenly he decided to start a boxing match with his brother, as they often took their fraternal exercise, and he gave him a punch under the elbow.

The comic Pietro raised his arm painfully, biting his lips, and would have immediately returned the quick-handed compliment, had his grandfather, on his part, not raised his cane with a real bear's growl.

"So, you think you're at the sheep pen, asses that you are? Cut it out, Paolo! Do and say something less stupid."

"All right then, let's sing a song, that one that goes, 'I went to the fair of Saint Gasta, the fair that comes in the spring.' "

And they would have sung it, had not a new event dampened their ardor and their incipient rivalry, pushing them to draw close to one another as if to defend themselves from a common danger.

For suddenly, everything around and inside the hospitable little house was movement, novelty, noise, and real life.

Comare Maria Giuseppa suddenly arrived, this time certainly not for a judicial controversy. She was no longer disguised as a man, but she was still covered with heavy clothes, with a black silk bonnet, and tied over it a handkerchief that seemed to have picked up all of the flowers and green stalks of the country road as a decoration. Around her mighty calves, on top of her high, elastic-sided shoes, she had fastened two shining spurs. After having led the horse under the little wellshed, making a sign of greeting to the chickens, she pulled down her full knapsack and carried it to the little stone bench next to the door. She had already seen the two youths in the kitchen, and she wrinkled her eyebrows which, in terms of being thick and unruly, rivaled those of Giordano. But her frown became absolutely warlike, aggressive, when she discovered the old man. He stared at her also in surprise, curious, and, finally, alarmed.

They did not know each other personally, but he knew very well about Maria Giuseppa Alivia, about her real wealth, her arrogance, and even her imbecile bastard nephew to whom all her stuff was promised. He, Felice Giordano, didn't give a fig (not to use the expression he really thought at that moment) about all those things. Still, he armed himself, without making a single movement. He armed himself like when he watched out for the thieves of his pigs, ready to wound and kill without mercy if they dared carry out their plans. He really did need to watch out for Maria Giuseppa; oh, much more than for the guitar-playing stranger. His fury grew when, after the mother ran with one leap to meet the guest, he saw Concezione get up and change her expression.

Deep down, she was glad about the arrival of the woman who would put an end to the other's unpleasant visit, but she did feel that the encounter would not be smooth, and she hardly knew whether to be amused or saddened. She remembered well Serafino's words, "You are like life, that awakens so many strivings and desires, and leaves everyone disappointed."

No, she did not want to disappoint; and above all, she didn't want to deceive anyone. But she felt a vague sense of vengeance against her illness and its consequent sufferings, to see those people disputing over something that did not exist. After having greeted the guest with reserved courtesy, repressing her first impulse to show disrespect for the Giordanos, she returned to her seat. She did not take up her work, but followed the others' scenes like a spectator. The youths and the grandfather had the good manners to greet the woman with nods of their heads, even if they did not stand up. She, who had already guessed what it was all about, thought she should attack them immediately and make them go away,

"My Comare Giustina," she said, leaning over to take off her spurs, "I brought you a little thing I would like to think Maria Concezione will appreciate. It's not what Maria Concezione deserves, she deserves all the treasures of the world, but . . . but . . . "

Giustina knew what sorts of little things she tended to bring as gifts, and was too much of a housewife and too good a housekeeper not to be glad about it. Still, she did not rush to bring in the knapsack, and that made the three men even more curious.

"So that's it," thought the old man maliciously. "To become friends with these little women you need to bring them gifts. I wouldn't have thought of it, but I'm still in time."

With patriarchal dignity he said, "I, too, raise a good piglet, for Comare Maria Giustina; she also deserves some treasure."

Pietro, though, free from his first embarrassment, wanted to be funny again, and said that as soon as they were in season, he would bring a little basket full of grasshoppers.

"The Hebrews ate locusts," said the guest seriously as she hung her spurs on a nail with a familiar air, "but we are baptized Christians, and we nourish ourselves with bread and holy food."

He was about to reply, but the woman pretended not to pay attention to him or the others, using the same tactic that old Giordano had used with Aroldo. And perhaps he remembered it, because, to better sting the guest and get back at her immediately, imitating her actions a bit, he turned to Concezione.

"To go back to our interrupted discussion," he said, "I tell you that that youth, that beanpole, that favorite suitor of yours . . . "

"Who? Who?" immediately replied the guest, now unable to stop herself. "You never tell me anything."

"But let him sing. The old man needs to joke. I don't have any suitors, favored or otherwise. That's enough of these stories."

But the old man was too unsettled to still not try to shoot a few arrows. When Giustina served the coffee, he pushed away the cup with disgust.

"Imagine that I would want this black water! I've already had three glasses of *acquavita*, and I drank them in good company, with Compare Francesco Marcello, the one who bought your blessed husband's land, and now plans to sell it because he wants to build a house for his grandsons who are studying to be lawyers and doctors. I really think he wants to sell it because these boys, who are orphans like mine, but from very different blood, are nibbling away at the patrimony. But this doesn't matter to us; what matters is that if you, Giustina, and you, Maria Concezione, don't want to redeem the land, as your blessed husband wished, I plan to buy it myself."

"Yes," thought Concezione, "with my money. Not on your life, old man."

Comare Giuseppa, sitting with her legs apart and with the little cup in both hands, now definitely paid attention to his words, and her eyes flashed like black pearls. But she addressed herself only to Giustina, and even measured the sound of her words.

"What? What? Is this what your husband said he wanted?"

"But let the old man tell the story; he really is in the mood to joke. Today is a holiday, and the *acquavita* is already running in streams in the tavern in town."

A blow from the old man's cane made the floor shake and the cat run away; but he did not go on, not to seem rude, and because the two women had turned completely towards each other and spoke to each other as though he were not there.

Giustina was informed about the health of her guest's husband and of the news up there in her village. She listened with reverence to the slightly vain answers with which Maria Giuseppa exaggerated the miseries of her native place to make her well-being and that of her household stand out better. She did this so much that Concezione began to be irritated and decided to talk with the Giordanos.

In the meantime, the knapsack remained outside. It must not have had any food in it because the cat, after sniffing it well, and scratching at the flowers and birds of embroidered wool on top of it, went off into the thicket of beans.

It was now hot, and nature was in full bloom. The new moss, like green velvet on which lay pearls of dew, covered the rocks and the corners of ground in the shade. The sharp smell of wild mint flavored the air. The sound of the church bells of the little town, with musical fluctuations like a dance, enhanced the joy and festivity of innocent things, while in the women's kitchen, apparent friends, seemingly without reason for hostility, consumed themselves with their empty cravings.

"Yes," repeated Comare Maria Giuseppa, pursing her prune-colored lips to make her words calmer, but at the same time sharper and more pungent, "my husband, thank God, is healthy and blooming like a pontiff. He doesn't move around much, even though his legs are healthy—but everyone goes to see him and keep him company: the parish priest, the doctor, the secretary, the mayor. The poor also go, to feel in his pockets. And he sits there in the middle of them all, like Solomon. He talks little and listens a lot, and it's smart. He doesn't give offense, nor does he take offense from anyone. In good weather, he sits under the portico of our house, a real verandah, you know, with a rustic roof and real columns cut from granite; out there there's the good air that comes down from the mountains and the sweeping view that opens your heart just to look at it. And he sits there just like Solomon, smoking his pipe, and many come, even from far away, to ask his advice and submit their questions for his upright judgment."

She would have liked to add that no, he wasn't foolish like those brutes who, like big apes, drag their grandsons behind them to entertain people. But she remembered certain observations of, in fact, her husband about her unruly tongue, and didn't add another word.

"And your house is like Solomon's," said Comare Giustina, fascinated but also a tiny bit in adoration, "full of treasures and every gift of God, and may he preserve them for you for a long time."

The old man wanted to grunt; he thought about his low house in the most central neighborhood of the little town, and almost glowered. Oh, Concezione would certainly prefer the house of the guest; but he also listened a bit enchanted, comforted only by the thought that the woman exaggerated the color of the pictures she painted.

"In the winter, rather, he stays in the kitchen—not in the kitchen where the oven is and they make bread, but in the one with the fireplace. It's big, and, I'm telling you, as beautiful as the assembly room in city hall. Yes, it's plastered, and has shiny tables and benches. And then, there are two fireplaces, because people's backs should also be warmed up when it's cold. When it snows and the men can't go to work, well then, they all come to our house. They play cards, and every now and then my husband gets up, very quietly, and goes to get a jug of wine. Ah, in this he's generous. He needs to see the people around him happy; and if some poor wretch looks at him like a hungry dog, he extends a hand to help him secretly."

"In short, we'll make him a saint," shot back the old man, and she turned a serious face to him as though he were speaking seriously.

"Oh, certainly, he'll go to heaven."

"Well then, best regards, and may he pray for us," he said, getting up.

He was indignant to have to leave like that, without reaching his goal. But seeing that both his grandsons, leaning towards Concezione as if to warm themselves at the fire of her body, smiled widely, showing their strong white teeth, he thought it would be good to leave them there. Maybe by themselves, spurred by the presence of the rival guest, they would be able to get on with it better, especially since, as he knew well, they had already begun to get seriously warmed up. Therefore, he motioned them to stay, and then left brusquely, leaving the door open.

And when he had left, a better sense of cordiality enlivened the bidders. After all, Comare Maria Giuseppa loved young people, and the two lads didn't seem so unpleasant to her. Just as the old man had been reminded of his gloomy house, so she was reminded of her illegitimate nephew, with eyes of a ram and a mouth almost always open like the beak of a bird waiting for food. Oh, the Lord divides the blessings of this earth in equal parts, and he is always just, even when he seems least to be. So she turned towards the group of young people and interrogated Pietro kindly, but he responded by returning to his diffident and mocking tone.

"I have two hundred sheep, all mine. They're not your flocks, but after all they're not two hundred nothings either. I get by. And then grandfather himself has a few things too. It's not your wealth . . . "

"Oh, stop it, boy," she said good naturedly. "You shouldn't tease old people. And besides, my lamb, you have riches few kings have."

"We got it," the other one interrupted, not without a spot of jealousy. "It's youth, which is also the beauty of the ass."

Pietro gave him a thump on the shoulders, at which Paolo straightened himself up and acted like he had swallowed a pebble.

But he was pretending, and he felt happy all the same. From the open door, through the shimmering lace of the trees, he saw a blue border of mountain and sky, and the far-off voice of the cuckoo spoke of secret places, of soft, shady corners of the forest, where it would have been infinitely sweet for the young suitors to kiss Maria Concezione. But for her, who had once more bent over her cloth that seemed to reflect its rough pallor on her face, the lament of the cuckoo opened up in her an unexpected void, cold and solitary. From time to time she even thought she heard the rocky rumblings of the explosives and then, reminding herself that it was a holiday, she asked herself where Aroldo was. With that woman? Or was he astray, a stranger among strangers, also surrounded by emptiness and solitude? Without lifting her face, while the two young men addressed themselves to the guest and joked with her as with a girl, she stuck her hand under her armpit, crossed the other hand over the folded arm and rested her chin there. She seemed to be asleep.

The gift offered by the guest this time would have seemed odd, except for the meaning that the two women immediately understood it to have, even though they took no pleasure in it. It was an ancient bed blanket, of wool that seemed to be silk, light and soft; if blown on, it puffed up like a veil. Rather than from silk, it seemed to have been woven from thread of feathers, and it took its color and weave from certain bird's feathers, gray, red, yellow, violet, blue, and black; while all around the border ran an archaic frieze, a fugue of little lambs, crosses, doves, and little branches of myrtle. It looked like, and really was, a tapestry. Concezione immediately thought, not without a certain tenderness, that since the precious blanket could not be used for her nuptial bed, it would be well and fittingly placed under the naked Christ during the days of the Holy Sepulchre.

She didn't say it. She accepted the strange and opulent gift, letting her mother somewhat roughly fold up the blanket as tightly as possible and place it on top of the other modest things in the chest in the bedroom. Maria Giuseppa did not stop talking, while with one foot up on the little bench, she tightened the strings of her blue cotton socks, showing legs as large and solid as a pig's trotters.

"And so those two young boars are courting you? They are not pretty, but they're not unlikeable either. But we need to melt them down and make a single one to get a proper Christian. I don't like the grandfather, though, may hell take him. He really is a boar, but one of those real ones that live among the thorns and nourish themselves with snakes. If looks could kill, I would be dead by now, under the dagger of his gaze. May the guardian angel free us from him."

"But no, he's not evil. He's a gentleman, one who grumbles but is incapable of hurting a lizard," truth-loving Giustina defended him. "Certainly, he loves his grandsons and tries to help them however he can."

"And what do you think of the young fellows?"

"I don't know—you should ask Maria Concezione."

"Maria Concezione, what do you think?"

"It's the first time I've seen them. I'm neither hot nor cold on them."

"Good," the guest approved, comforted, "As far as looks are concerned, my Costante is stronger and more handsome than they are. He's simple, it's true, but you can make whatever you want out of him."

"I won't make anything," said Concezione, with a still sadness. "I'll say it again: I will never marry. If you want to remain our friend, we will always be glad, but let's not talk about these things anymore."

Fate still had it that no one would believe her intentions, and Maria Giuseppa thought instead of that damned stranger the old man had mentioned. Concezione must be in love with him. Something was stopping her from marrying him; but because of her love for him she would not accept other marriage proposals. It was necessary to eliminate the unwelcome stranger, to make him go away, get him out of the way by any possible means.

During the meal, she tried to get to know and understand better the story of Aroldo. The women gave her no satisfaction, and so she decided to make an investigation on her own. She said she had to go see an acquaintance in town, and she went off with long, decisive steps. She came back an hour later, but she must have found out little, because she had the dissatisfied air of one who has made a futile trip; and with this air she remounted her horse and left.

"Mary, Mother of God, make them leave me alone," Concezione prayed, kneeling at the foot of the altar. "I only ask to be able to live as long as my mother is alive, and not to make her suffer. Afterwards, do with me what you want. I am ready for anything; pain does not frighten me, only mortal sin does. And all these people surrounding my bones like hungry dogs make me sin with hatred, anger, vanity. Yes, vanity, since sometimes I delude myself by thinking it's my body that arouses desire and rivalry, while they are all guided by petty personal interests. And if they knew that a terrible illness, the worst of all, was lurking like a poisonous snake in my poor breast, they would flee me like they flee lepers and the possessed. Most Holy Mary, make them leave me in peace, like an old woman who has nothing in the world but a meter of ground on which to die, and under which to be buried."

She said three Hail Marys, since the Mother of God does not deny her comfort to those who greet her as a faithful friend. Meanwhile, the dense perfume of the velvety purple iris with which Concezione had decorated the altar, and the smell of the bushes, the cyclamen, and the wild morning glory that wafted in from the window open to the valley, reached deep into her soul. And those volcanic signals of the explosions, which had started again early that morning, shook her completely, threatening to break her heart and send it into the air in fragments, like the mountain rock. She prayed more about this than about the persecution of her suitors; the real persecution was in her blood, in her tenacious love of life, in her fear of sickness, pain, death.

She stayed under the altar for a long time, folding herself little by little on her knees into a crouch. She seemed to find a refuge, a hiding place from herself in the little church, still cold and gray, where the spiders had also taken refuge, and the naked, yellow Christ on his black cross, with his face turned towards the left, seemed vexed by his crown of thorns. She felt a maternal piety for him, more than for the Christ Child of the restless feet that seemed to try their first steps over the moon and the stars. She would have liked to take down that resigned and yet suffering dark Christ, lay him out on the new bed covering, make him rest among the flowers as he had during the days of the Holy Sepulchre.

And suddenly, by association, she thought more intensely and of her own free will about Aroldo; it again seemed to her that the Christ resembled him in some way.

"Mary, Mother of God, remove him from my thoughts. Make him go far away, to the other side of the world, so that I won't hear about him anymore. And keep him happy, free of sin, good and pure just as I have known him."

But his lively, true image—the almost silver wave of his hair, the imploring blue of his eyes, and most of all his mouth, sensual and chaste at the same time—oppressed her day and night, even in her dreams, indeed, especially in her dreams, when her willpower did not rein in her still young and avid senses.

Often, there was mixed into her thoughts the memory, the cloudy image, of "the other one." Then a feeling of mortal anxiety overcame her, as if the dead man had risen up from hell, having become the essence of the devil, of evil, of endless pain. She awakened all in a sweat, and to calm herself she thought, turning back to reality, that her suffering was perhaps an expiation; God would keep it in mind when it was time to make the great journey.

Another almost diabolical figure was the primary physician of the hospital; he personified for her the first judge who had pronounced her condemnation. Sometimes she thought about going to see him as he had ordered, but she was almost terrified of him, she feared that he would announce a recurrence of the disease near at hand, a slow but not remote death. And she wanted to live: for her mother, she said, but really out of the simple instinct for living. What do the love, lineage, excessive food we ask of life matter when the very bread of life is enough to make us happy and to talk to God? Concezione had not studied; she only had read her missal; but she was intelligent, and solitude and atavism increased in her every day like in the mountain shepherds, a primordial but judicious view of life that was philosophical and almost stoic. She understood very well that the relationship between her illness and her love was almost an attachment, a vow, an obstacle like so many others; and that she had to fight with her senses, dreams, with the very instincts that the obstacle awakened in her. Like many refined people, she felt, deep down, a joy in, a taste for, pain.

One Monday her mother had gone to wash clothes in the stream, now running low but still sufficiently full. Concezione hoped that no one would come to bother her. She sat in the shade of the house with her needle, the shirts of Aroldo's companion, and the greetings of the far-away explosions. But instead the old pseudodoctor dropped by, brushing through the little gate, his overcoat all buttoned up as though the winter were still alive. When the weather allowed, he often took walks in those parts, every now and again stopping and bending over to look at the ground as though catching sight of some lost object, but not burdening himself by picking it up.

Instead, there would be a lizard quivering through the grass like a little fish in the waves, or a group of ants around a tiny well they had dug, or a family of little red flowers, or even a simple if marvelous drop of dew that in its void reflected the dazzling mystery of the universe.

"He probably hasn't eaten in two days," thought Concezione. Going to meet him, she made him come in, and brought him out a good chair.

"How's it going? How's it going?" he said, fixing her with a gaze somewhere between beatific and sad, the way he had earlier looked at the drop of dew. Everything in this world was still miraculous for him. The same type of marvel felt by a child who sees things for the first time, but does not know how to explain them, who would like to touch things with a finger, but doesn't dare to out of fear, not fear of destroying them, but of being pricked by them. This is why they had thrown the phlebotomist out of the community of men of true science, for whom there are no mysteries. And he still wandered along the paths of life, like a young boy who ran away from home for fear of being punished, but is happy to wander, doing nothing; even at the cost of feeling hunger.

"How are you, Doctor?" Concezione ventured. And seeing him move his small head like a fledgling waiting for food, she wondered what she could offer him without offending his dignity: not wine, at that hour, and there was too little coffee. Then she remembered that she had some cocoa and some nice big cookies, and she waited for the right moment to fix him a nice cup of chocolate and offer it to him with well-bred courtesy. He did not take his gaze from her; his milky eyes lit up with that spark of comfort she knew so well; and she too was comforted.

"I find you a bit run down, Concezione," he finally said. "But then, it's springtime. Spring is fatal to women. Like the earth, in this season women need to flower, enjoy, be fertile. Love is the best pollen for them. Everything goes well when there is love: nothing else in life counts, since life itself is the essence, the beginning and the end of love. If you, my dear friend, had married ten years ago, by now you would have three or four children here around you to keep company with the flowers, the birds, and above all, with your heart. But maybe you paid attention to other empty things in life, and so now you waste away, you are consumed slowly, like an almond that has dried up inside its shell before ripening."

She remembered her first love, her involuntary crime, and in her heart she agreed with the old man. But now that the sun made things bright and clean she didn't want to abandon herself to her ghosts. So, with a smile that showed all of her still intact teeth, she said, "The dried almond is also good. In fact, it's better than the fresh almond; they make sweets out of it. But I am old," she added immediately, so as not to be misunderstood, "too old; and when it's too old, the almond goes bad."

"No, dear friend, you are lying to yourself. I only have to look in your eyes. You're like a gypsy masquerading as a nun. And so, leaving theory, we come to reality. Confide in me, consult with me—I am still good enough to give you a few prescriptions."

This time he had added a foppish cane to his other elegances. With it he made windmills in the air; he especially loved to toss it up and catch it, with youthful dexterity, between his fingers. And Concezione, who had at first almost truly wanted to confide in him and tell him about her secret torment, seeing him so intent on that ridiculous game, took on a comically false and sentimental tone, telling him that, yes, she was in love, but with one who could not marry, a man who already had a wife and family far away. And thinking about Aroldo's companion, the one for whom she was sewing shirts, she threw herself into his role: she described him, making him more beautiful, younger, so that in the end she laughed at her truly amusing invention.

"You are taking me for a ride, my soul. I know that laborer: he's an old man, worse than me. But love has no age," he said, stopping the game with his cane. Stretching out his small yellow hand, on which the veins looked like leeches swimming under the wrinkled skin, he tried to touch her.

She shuddered with repugnance, and thought, then, not even the dead respected her. Now she wanted to get back at him. Moving away from him on the bench, she said, "No, he's not an old man. He's young; in fact, he's much younger than I am, one of those who can eat almonds shell and all. And it's not true that he's married. He's free, he's handsome, he's healthy—and good. He has hair like golden silk, and eyes and a mouth like flowers—look, like those flowers there, the cornflower and the peony. Actually, his mouth is even more beautiful; it's like a ripe red plum, when it breaks open and drips honey. And he's tall."

"And he's betrayed you, you mean."

"With whom? How do you know?"

"Well, I don't know, exactly. With another woman, I suppose. There are many pretty girls in our town who wait only for the man who will kiss them. They also have mouths made just for this, like ripe fruit waiting to be sucked. It's fair that it should be like this: it's nature. If you are so finicky, like the prickly pear that has to be cut out of its spiny skin with a knife to be enjoyed, it's only fair that your young man should turn elsewhere, especially if he's a stranger. I once knew a soldier, a boy from the north, who wanted to eat a prickly pear, and not knowing that it should be peeled, bit into it spines and all. He came to me with a mouth burning like a lighted stove, and it did for a good while. So your stranger goes for the apples, and the other pretty, pleasant fruit. And then, foreigners are famous for betraying women; sometimes they do it innocently. They love two or three at a time and pay no attention to quality. Oh, as far as that goes, our native men also don't go for subtlety, and often the trashiest woman, if she is versed in the amorous arts, ensnares them like the most astute fox is ensnared by the hidden trap."

"That's not the case, that's not the case," she said, now thinking that the old man was referring to Aroldo. "My case is different. It's about the fact that I have never had luck in love. It's destiny, luck, bad luck."

"Words. We make our own luck. If I had been shrewder, if I had taken care of my clients, if I had also bled the pockets of my sick people, I would have kept my prestige high and now I wouldn't be like an old unemployed laborer. Instead, I have

always been honest and generous. If a bleeding wasn't necessary, I didn't do it, and if I didn't know well enough the illness
for which the good people ran to me in faith, I sent them to
a doctor with a diploma. Once a wealthy woman came to me
from a mountain village; she was afraid she had a cancer, and
at any price she wanted me to operate on her in secret since in
her village the disease was shameful, like leprosy. I refused. She
didn't have anything more than a nervous illness, fixations,
phobias. Well then, she went to another, who cut off a piece of
her breast and earned a thousand scudi, and then he told the
story and laughed. The world, my dear, is made of scoundrels
and imbeciles. So, what about your blond boy?"

Concezione trembled; she seemed to be held tight in the
grip of an invisible hand. But it wasn't Aroldo's, that poor hand
burned from work and timid like the hand of a child. It was the
hand of an illusion, the illusion that the doctor was speaking
the truth, that his example could be adapted to her case: that
the doctors at the hospital had tricked her and that her illness
was just a painful illusion of her mind.

So she waited for the old man to give some other examples,
but he was already rambling. Among other things he told her
about how, as a boy, he had believed that there was a long
subterranean passage between the little Church of Solitude and
a grotto down in the valley to the north, a steep, bare, and
uninhabited place.

"As people say, your grandfathers and great grandfathers,
may the Lord have forgiven them, used it for their lovely un-
dertakings. They entered the passageway from a trapdoor under the altar of the church, went through the passage, came out
through the grotto, and took themselves off like errant knights
in search of riches. And they brought the booty back to the
grotto, where they kept sheep with their throats cut and other
provisions they accumulated, as if in a refrigerator."

Flaring slightly, Concezione said, "Let me point out for
one thing that this little church was built by my grandfather.
No one has ever accused him of anything but being too good
and scrupulous."

"Humpf," sneered the other. "did you ever know your grandfather? No; so then, forget it. Your father, sure, I don't deny it, he was a gentleman, a worker, religious, honest; and your mother, too, is a biblical woman. You, my friend, have taken a bit from both branches; you're like the fruit of a grafted tree, that still retains a bit of a wild taste. You are good and wicked at the same time. You are the true daughter of Eve—you also wanted to eat the apple, and if you don't do it, it's because you feel the terror of punishment still alive in your mother's skin. And so, going back to the story of the hidden passage, no one said that it began right in the church: your ancestors were too superstitious to let themselves down in the well of their own iniquity directly under the eyes of the Madonna. But the land around here was all theirs: the woods came down to here, and they pastured goats and pigs here. Their cabin probably stood right here, where we sit like two innocent doves. Or maybe the cabin of those brave scoundrels was over there by that rock, and the trapdoor began there, well hidden by dirt and dry leaves."

"You tell a beautiful tale; but tell it to the hens—they are right there."

In fact, they could see the hens inside the reed fence, black and white, blond, or tiger-striped, with their sultan of the red crest in the middle like a poppy. A few of them, standing behind the hedge with a foot in the air and looking with one eye only, really did seem to be listening to the doctor's story.

"They used to tell scary stories about your illustrious ancestors in those days: a little boy who came all the way up here looking for blackberries disappeared and was never found. It seems he saw them lift the trapdoor; at any rate, he was never found. The cries of his mother were heard in town for weeks on end; then she died with a broken heart. Still, I don't believe in curses, not even from a mother whose son was killed as a child. Bull! It's God who has spread curses around, on earth and on men. We still don't know very well the real reason why, but it's certain that pain and evil are natural laws, like storms, war, death."

"Talk to me about something happier," begged Concezione, still listening to him willingly.

But he no longer remembered what happiness was, what makes people laugh. On the other hand, he was, in his own way, entertaining himself that day with the tale of the subterranean passage, with the deeds of Concezione's ancestors, and most of all with the impression he made on his listener.

"Well, sometimes your venerated great-grandfathers—since you don't want us to touch your grandfather, we'll leave him out of it—your venerated great-grandfathers also amused themselves. Never mind the story of the priest who was made to sit on the burning tripod: it was, perhaps a seat worthy of him. Let's talk about the day when they invited a friend to a banquet and gave him a roast from a calf they had stolen from him the day before; and this time they stole the calf just to play that trick on their friend. They couldn't have played a more innocent trick than that one. But the good part came later, when they got the friend drunk and let him down through the trapdoor, so that when he sobered up, he thought he had been buried alive. But, by groping, he managed to find the entrance to the grotto, and he was the first to laugh about the trick."

"Oh, that's enough, Doctor," said Concezione. "In any case, I don't believe in these nonsensical stories; they're not worthy of you. Leave them to old Giordano."

"He's a good one too! He also has a subterranean passage, in his rocky soul where he can hide the most ghastly dreams, but without putting them into effect. Times have changed, and now we have our good Don Calogero, who doesn't love jokes of any sort."

Don Calogero was the sergeant of the Carabinieri, feared and loved by all the people. And the doctor, who knew that he was under his surveillance, spoke well of him, and said that the good soldier's vigilance, without seeming to, reached all the way to the little church and to its solitary inhabitants, something that did not cheer up Concezione. She felt sad, and asked herself if perhaps there were not curses from the mother whose child had been killed still bearing down on her. It was futile that the doctor, upon leaving, told her that he had made up all of his gossip, and advised her to enjoy herself and to make love.

Instead, in her fantasies, she thought that she would like to do some pious deed: help the sick, wash and dress the dead, help the poor, take some orphan into her home. She even thought about her lost sister with the desire to go and visit her, to save her from evil. She was ready to divide her inheritance with her; but her mother was a wise and practical woman, whose presence kept her from foolish acts.

And so summer came, a glittering of hillsides covered with ripe barley, wheat already in ears, pastures turning golden, the noisy song of the nightingales that had finished nesting, and of blackbirds that imitated them, almost mocking their sentimental refrain. In the garden, the cherry tree wept large tears of blood, and the last artichokes opened their hard purple flowers. The rest of the vegetation was already a bit decomposed, a dry decomposition which still at night had a passionate perfume like burned juniper; it resembled that of Concezione's heart. She felt tired and listless, as though she had worked at breaking rocks with the road laborers, and everything to her was, or seemed, indifferent, useless, futile. The rumbling of the explosives had stopped, and with it she felt that Aroldo had gone far away from her forever. But in the meantime, the road work progressed towards the town, and standing at the little wall, she could see it.

One day the worker whose modest linens she sewed and mended returned, and he told her that, contrary to her hopes, Aroldo was always in town, at the house of that woman. He walked kilometers and lost whole nights to go see her, and he spent his savings to give her gifts so that people wouldn't think his attachment selfish.

"I swear to God, he seems bewitched. He's thin as a herring, and looks older than I do. That woman is cunning though; up to now she's refused him in order to make him even more foolish. And so it's almost certain to turn out that in the end they'll go away together."

Cold and hostile, yet with a vague relief, she said, "Good luck. Have a good trip."

And each time the memory, or as she put it, the temptation, of the young stranger came back to her mind, sometimes in an almost tangible way, swollen with anguish and jealousy, she tried to squash it like you squash a troublesome insect. But the insect was reborn more lively and stinging, and she was totally tormented. She didn't want to pray anymore; the Hail Marys came out of her mouth all withered while her thoughts wandered far away. She didn't eat, she grew thin, she wanted to close herself ever more into her circle of death and vanish like the little clouds of summer.

Her mother took great pains to make good food for her: sweets, shortbread, and eggnogs. She left it all untouched and ate bitter onions and raw tomatoes.

In July there was the feast of the patron saint of the small city, Saint Cyril Martyr.* The peasants had already harvested the barley, and the shepherds had sold their wool and lambs; and so the celebration, which lasted three days, with pealing of bells, processions, fireworks, and sale of wine and ice cream, became a small revel, and everyone competed to cut a good figure. And there were no stingy people; indeed, for the occasion, the poorest became the biggest spenders. People arrived on foot and on horseback by the new road and the old ones, from up on the mountains and down in the valleys, as guests and as pilgrims, and even as people who wanted to entertain themselves in order to commemorate the martyrdom of the saint.

And so it happened that Comare Maria Giuseppa also arrived, and Concezione saw with annoyance, if not with fear,

---

*The Feast of Saints Cyril and Methodius, Greek missionaries to the Slavs, is celebrated in July, but Deledda may be thinking of the child St. Cyril, martyr, whose feast day is May 29.

that the proud woman had in tow a young man on horseback, well dressed in an almost sporty outfit: a jacket with a belt, pants tucked into gaiters of gray cloth, a new visored cap, also gray, that shaded a ruddy, hairless face with features like a Greek statue. His mouth was also beautiful: protruding, sensual, swollen with blood. But his eyes lay still under black eyebrows, one higher and thicker than the other, they were dark, round, of a muddy brown color, with the whites streaked with red: they looked like the eyes of a dog about to become angry.

Giustina, who went to the gate, felt a certain relief that the guests were not to stay with them. They were going to another acquaintance in town and would return in the afternoon for a visit. Concezione hid herself and thought about pretending to be ill to escape persecution. She felt truly ill, from the heat, from boredom, from sadness. Comare Maria Giuseppa had left a box with a honey cake ornamented with flowers and little birds of sugar and gold foil. Concezione intended to send it to Serafino, but in the meantime, she placed it inside the chest on top of the famous blanket that gave her a funereal melancholy every time she smelled the scent of wool colored with vegetable dyes, and reminded her of the Holy Sepulchre. Then she gathered her courage and told herself that it was necessary to be polite to those two out of consideration for her mother, and because of the ancient law of hospitality. But, with the excuse that she had a toothache, she disguised herself as an old woman, with a black kerchief pulled on above her eyes and wrapped up all the way to her mouth. She looked at herself in the mirror, and she would have felt satisfied by her mask, if her eyes had not appeared, in that monastic frame, larger, beautiful with all the mystery of her soul, sad, and in exile on the earth. She lowered her eyelashes and tried to hide herself better, to escape the pernicious ambush; but as the hour passed, she felt an oppression, a poison of hatred against that madwoman Comare Maria Giuseppa and her worthy nephew. She went to pick a bouquet of pink oleanders for the altar, from the only plant that had grown up spontaneously in the back of the garden, and she was delighted to drink in its perfume like a slightly bitter liquor. It was a perfume that seemed to come from far away, from the river, from the valley, from her girlhood; and memories that she believed had been definitively squashed and had gone away like birds go from a place where they no longer find either water or food arose again, almost rapaciously, in her heart. Yes, the oleander had been there for many years, she had known it since she was a girl, with all those leaves that looked like green spears, that grew rusty in the sun, and the flowers of a vivid pink, folded against the little wall above the valley, as if they were listening with nostalgia to the sound of the distant water from which they too had been exiled. At that time she stood for hours folded up against the little wall, in the shade of the flowering plant, listening, without knowing it, to the voices of her past, of her blood, of her passionate and dreamy lineage, dreamy even in its cruelty and misery. And behold, the figure of the bronzed boy with eyes of a lovesick leopard that comes through the grass and the rocks, agile and silent, his mouth and gums the color of the oleanders, his breath slightly bitter and fresh like theirs. And he calls her softly, inviting her to jump over the little wall and hide herself with him among the bushes, with the mated lizards and the cold snakes.

If she had really listened to him and to the voices of nature, he would not have robbed, would not have hanged himself for her, and perhaps the evil that now gnawed at her would not have come. But she was rich, with the money of the robberies of her ancestors, and the curse of that gold persecuted her. She had a glimpse of this demonic punishment in the eyes of the imbecile, and the eyes of the boy now came back into her mind like those of an archangel whom she had sent to hell.

"God, God, deliver me from evil," she said out loud. Then she went to place the flowers below the impassive little Madonna, who seemed only to care about not letting her restless child slide out of her bosom.

In spite of the heat outside, the little church was cool, with its usual cellar smell mixed with the smell of the aromatic herbs along the bank under the half-open little window.

Concezione drew near this opening and saw the rocky valley and, on the horizon, the limestone mountains that seemed still white with snow. The path that Maria Giuseppa and her imbecile nephew had taken snaked like the bed of a dried up stream, and lost itself among the juniper bushes. It had something of ambiguity, of brigandry about it, that made one think of the subterranean passage hinted at by the fanciful phlebotomist. Nevertheless, she would have liked to have found this passage, if for no other reason than to hide herself in it if she needed to. She roamed about the little church pressing the dusty pavement here and there with her feet; she also looked around and under the altar, she probed the walls. In the end she blushed and was ashamed because it seemed to her that the little Madonna, up high on her half moon, was looking at her with cold irony. "How can it be, Maria Concezione, silly creature, that you remain up here, on top of a well full of mortal sins? Oh no, I would have been gone a while ago; and you, silly, go, return to your work, stop your lazy fantasizing."

And she returned to the little house and prepared the chairs, the coffee, the cookies for the visitors. She wished that Madama Peperona and the other beggars would come too, so that she could give them alms. She swept and watered down in front of the house, ran after and shut up in the pen a hen that had escaped and wandered about as foolishly as she herself did. From the town wafted the sounds of bells, the shots of the target shooting contest, soft music of an accordion. They seemed unreal, as if they came from a town that did not exist except in her fantasy, like sounds that produce the buzzing in a sick ear. No one was around, and the little church seemed lost in the harshest solitude of the mountains. Then all of a sudden she had a sort of hallucination; or rather she seemed to dream one of her usual daydreams. A man dressed in the color of granite was seated right on a boulder above the garden; they were almost indistinguishable. He appeared to be asleep, or to be one of the illusory appearances that outline profiles on rocks or in the clouds. There were no clouds, even though the sky was lightly veiled by haze from the heat, purple striped with red. The man held his hands tightly between his knees, and his head, hidden by a gray cap, leaned on his chest. What was he doing up there, all alone, almost dominating the landscape like a master who watches over his land? He seemed to have fled from the uproar of the fair, but the noise, the music, the sound of the bells had put him to sleep like a restless child. Concezione recognized him, more than anything from her own agitation. It was Aroldo. And she was afraid that Comare Maria Giuseppa and her nephew would see him and think badly of him. She would have liked to run up there and awaken him and beg him to go; but what right did she have to do this? And besides, she was afraid to approach him. That day everything oppressed her, gave her a sense of anguish, like when a spring storm approaches. Then she shrugged her shoulders: maybe, yes, it would be better for those two to see him and to think badly of him and also of her, and so be done with annoying her.

But Giustina had also become aware of him and without saying anything, she set out on the path that led up the hill. The path passed under the boulders on which Aroldo was seated, and she, who had good legs and a strong heart, climbed all the way to just below the wild pedestal that served as a throne for the sentimental stranger. From there she could see the road that led to the town; and she sighed, because she too had been afraid that people would become aware of the presence of Aroldo and would gossip, and above all that the rumors of the spiteful would reach the Giordanos, about whom she still nourished some hope. She also was not enthusiastic about Comare Maria Giuseppa and her nephew, but it was better that they not see Aroldo in the vicinity of the little church. So she called to the young man, first softly, then more loudly. She came right to the edge of the boulder, and she saw that behind the shoulders of the sleeper, in a hollow in the rock, was a guitar that also looked asleep, turned over like a yellowish tortoise. And, if she had known about literature, good Giustina might have compared the youth to a wandering troubadour who, after crossing the dark forests of the mountains, rested before starting out again on his capricious journey. But she thought instead about her daughter's reputation, and since her arms couldn't reach Aroldo, she carefully took the guitar and stretched it towards him. The strings vibrated, and this moan shook the man who seemed to be overtaken by an enchantment rather than by sleep. His large blue eyes, surrounded by shadows, stared at the woman without recognizing her; and she too struggled to see again in him the fresh boy of a few months ago. He was thin, as if sucked out by an illness. His lips were gray, his hair, once soft and golden, was short and coarse like mown stubble. Finally, since he was leaning forward, she smelled the stench of pipe tobacco and *acquavita*; and with true pain she became aware that he was completely drunk.

On a superstitious impulse, she also thought about the curse of the bastard daughter of her dead husband. She had tainted the young man, only because he loved Concezione. She was making him die slowly, and he would end by coming apart like the shell of a boat abandoned on the waves. And he would also lose himself before God.

Almost kneeling, she said, "Son, dear little son, don't you recognize me? I am Concezione's mother."

He yawned, leaving his mouth open almost as though he couldn't close it. He seemed to say, "And what do you and this Concezione matter to me? I don't know you. Leave me in peace—I was so comfortable."

"I was so comfortable," he grumbled with the vague voice of drunkenness in reply to her insistence. "Don't break my balls. Go away, you old bitch."

"My little son," she insisted in anguish, "come down. At least stretch out here below, in the shade. They can see you; they can steal your wallet. There are so many vagrants around; they've come to the fair."

Instinctively, he touched his jacket, to reassure himself that his wallet was there; and the idea that they might steal it seemed to convince him to come down from the boulder, sliding down clumsily and ripping his trousers. Without Giustina's help he would have fallen and hurt himself. She helped him with patience and strength. She pulled down the guitar, and was not content until she saw him stretched out on the grass under the rocks, invisible from the garden and the path. She placed the instrument next to him and decided to keep an eye on him so that he wouldn't really be robbed.

Returning home, she said softly, "Concezione, that wretch is back there, dead drunk and unconscious. What should we·do?"

She didn't know either. Wait for the drunkenness to pass; wait until some boy came as far as the little church and ask him to go call Aroldo's companion to watch out for the wretch and take him home. There wasn't any alternative. But no one passed by; they were all at the fair, attracted like bees to the odor of wine and sweets. Their guests also made them wait, and the sun was already turning red, divesting itself of its incandescent rays. An almost dark peace fell with the sunset: the limestone mountains were colored as though lit by a fire, while the hot shade of the valley climbed from rock to rock, through the garden, and seemed to take refuge in the oak forest for the night. The perfume of the yew mixed with that of the oleander, with a sweetness of an aromatic drug that went to your head. And the wet down clearing gave off an unexpected coolness that reminded Concezione of the ices sold by the traveling vendors. She awaited her guests with her thoughts always on the drunken wretch, and with the fear that he would awaken and come down, perhaps to make an imprudent scene, and she felt her disgust and hatred for them grow. In fact, everything, except for her mother, seemed to her wrapped up in her restless and evil feeling: why couldn't they leave her in peace?

She sat wearily on the little bench, while the old woman, followed by the cat as if by a little dog, watered the fragrant tomatoes stingily, since the water in the well was already scarce. "To go back," Concezione sighed, "to those hot evenings full of temptation and illusion of my earliest youth! To listen to the whistle of the dark boy, under the wall red with the sunset. To flee with him, sin with him, love, suffer, have children and work for them!" The nurse in that damned hospital had told her that if she had nursed a child the disease would not have come; and the boy with eyes like dark stars would not have minted counterfeit money and would not have hanged himself like Judas.

"But we never know anything for sure in this life. Away! Go away, evil memories, useless laments, dark temptations! Go away with the bats that flutter like pieces of burned paper over the roof of the church."

It grew late. Perhaps those two, foolishly bewitched by the fair, wouldn't come back that day. And that other one, asleep like a snake there behind the rocks, would spend the night up there, and also keep her from sleeping peacefully.

Irritated, she called her mother, "I say we should try to wake up that idiot. If they find him there he could get in trouble."

"Let's wait a little longer, in case Maria Giuseppa should arrive unexpectedly."

"A curse on her and her imbecile nephew! Ugh! Ugh!"

She fanned her face with the corner of her apron. She would have liked to have gone to bed and to stretch herself out nude between the cool sheets. As evening fell the heat increased. Not one blade of grass moved. The stones gave off a heat like banked coals; and as the oppression grew, a crimson flame appeared on top of the mountain: the rising moon.

By its light, with the trampling of the horses those two finally arrived. To tell the truth, the nephew walked with an elastic step, since he had shoes with rubber heels and his movements were instinctively feline, like a young beast who stalks the female with whom he wants to mate. Concezione immediately understood his animal instinct towards her. She understood it immediately, just from the way the young man turned to close the little wooden gate as if to prevent escape, and then from the way he looked her all over, avidly, from her legs to her breast, stopping there with eyes like a vampire. She wanted to yell at him: "You wretch, you are looking at the flowers of death!"

She would have liked to scare him, like he had scared her. She thought, "If this ferocious beast discovers Aroldo, he really is capable of squashing him like a garter snake."

And because of this fear, she tried to be courteous and happy. She insisted that the guests come inside, into the room that had been cleaned and set in order for the occasion. She even closed the door with the excuse that there were mosquitoes outside. But she noticed that the young man, who had been to have his shining black hair trimmed and perfumed, first looked at himself in the mirror, and then could not stop staring at the bed with his hideous, red-veined eyes. And when she went into the kitchen to get the coffee pot, she ground her teeth with anger and disgust.

They talked about the fair. Comare Maria Giuseppa insisted that Concezione go with them the next day to see the procession and the fireworks. To seduce her, she promised to take her to sit at one of the little tables of the caffè, on the sidewalk of the boulevard, to get an ice cream—the real stuff, not the well water and worn out lemons that the traveling vendors sell.

"Then we'll bring you back home, with this beautiful moon that resembles a bonfire of Saint John's Day, and we will all be happy. Speak, Costante," she said to her nephew. "You invite her too."

He showed his perfect teeth, that in the light of the oil lantern seemed to be of porcelain. He snarled and brought his fist to his temple. Finally, he said, "Either Maria, or pow!"

"What does he mean?" asked Giustina, while Comare Maria Giuseppa laughed with a lioness's roar. But Concezione did not laugh when she found out what that "boy" meant by that gesture and those words.

"He means he'll shoot himself if he doesn't have Maria Concezione."

And those were the only words he used to express the bestial passion for poor Maria Concezione that his aunt had inoculated into his blood with her promises and suggestions.

Fortunately, they left soon, without accepting an invitation to return the next day to have a bite with the two women. Giustina accompanied them a way down the road towards the town, while Concezione sat down again on the little bench illuminated by the moon.

Yes, there was a mosquito or two, but they were harmless. The crickets sang, and their vibrant screeching blended in with the perfume of the yew and the oleander and with the light of the moon trembling on every leaf. Concezione's heart ached. She didn't want to go in to dinner; indeed, she answered her mother's insistent invitations crossly. Her mother irritated her even more when, having eaten, she came outside again and began to pick her teeth.

"Let's go to bed, daughter, and let's lock the door well," she said after a minute. "Who knows if that unfortunate one is still back there or if he woke up and went away."

"Let's hope he dropped dead; he and all those like him."

"Let's hope not," the mother calmly insisted. "At any rate, Concezione, it's better to go to bed and lock the door well."

"Not even in your dreams. I don't want to go to sleep, and I am not afraid of anyone, even if they should come to kill me."

Her mother made the sign of the cross, but she clenched the toothpick between her fingers, and Concezione became even more irritated.

"Do me a favor, Mamma: you go to bed. I'll stay here a bit longer, until I calm my nerves. This isn't the first time."

She raised her voice and picked up a club that was leaning against the wall. Her mother had the impression that she wanted to beat someone, and she started to laugh.

"You are right to be angry, my soul. Comare Maria Giuseppa is raving mad, and she can make a salami or an omelet from her nephew—don't take it so much to heart."

But Concezione was angry at that other man, the drunk one. She wanted to go wake him up with blows from her club and drive him away like a skunk caught stalking the hen house. "Go, you miserable wretch, go back to your loose woman. What did you come to do here in the holy shadow of the little Madonna? Go, you damned stranger, and a curse on the hour you came to give me work, and on the one who taught me to sew men's clothing!"

She thought about the teacher who had taught her about needle and scissors. She was a very beautiful woman who also lived alone in a solitary house surrounded by a courtyard with high walls. It was said that a rich man, married and with children, was her lover. One day the woman died. Her heirs demolished the stairs in front of the house for certain restorations, and found underneath them little bones of newborn babies, probably suffocated by their mother.

"And she seemed a saint, and she spoke evangelically, like a preacher from the altar. Virgin Mary, have pity on us, pray for all us sinners now and in the hour of our death. And, yes, pray too for that unlucky man asleep under the rocks."

She recited many Hail Marys until she became sleepy. Then she thought she would make her mother happy by coming to bed, leaving the little Madonna to watch over Aroldo. But when she heard her mother's snoring, she took off her shoes, and like a sleepwalker, she opened the chest and took out the blanket given to her by that raving lunatic Maria Giuseppa. Odors of lavender and honey cake came out of the chest. Concezione almost took the cake too, but she had her hands full with her shoes and the blanket, so she let the lid fall closed. She felt like she was dreaming, a lucid and precise dream, like those that take a more vivid shape than reality.

She went outside, but not through the kitchen, since she had barred the door. First she went into the sacristy, illuminated by the orange light of the moon above the high window, and she put her shoes back on. Then she went into the little church, and by the gleam of the little oil lamp that always burned in the niche, she went to the door and opened it halfway. A wave of cricket song washed over her. The moon stretched a silver curtain over the clearing, and on the horizon the sky still had the reflection of the fireworks from the fair.

It was as bright as the dawn. On the ground, the shadow of every stalk, every little stone was visible. It looked like everything was stripped bare, with its clothing stretched out in front of it, to enjoy the freshness of the night. And she walked cautiously, so as to disturb not even a blade of grass, so as not to disturb the almost hallucinatory dream of that marvelous night. After she passed the little church, when she brushed against a rock covered with a down of moss, she jumped like she had touched a drowsy animal. She still had the handkerchief tied around her head, with her mouth covered, and she looked like she really was suffering from a sharp toothache. She stumbled and made a bit of noise, and the valley around her resounded like the explosives were sounding again. But she took courage; after all, she was going to do a good deed, to see whether that man, that orphan, that son of nobody, that man with no country and no peace, was alive or dead. She discovered him easily by the guitar gleaming in the moonlight. Both of them, the man and the instrument, were watched over by their shadows. More than anything, since Aroldo's face was covered by his cap, she recognized him by this cap, by his shoes, and by one hand that seemed like the hand of a corpse, also resting on the glove of his shadow.

A forceful, almost wild, pity, like the pity that moves birds of prey to help and try to save their own when in danger, melted her. Her acidified blood sweetened; she felt it flowing like a generous wine, from her feet to her ears. She wanted to kneel down next to the young man, shake him out of his bad dream, say to him, "Listen, Aroldo, we are both unhappy people, but if you have the strength, we could live like brother and sister, like the birds of the same species who are too old to mate any longer."

But she knew enough about men, and about herself, not to abandon herself to her romanticisms. And just as well, since she had brought the famous blanket to cover Aroldo, to save him from the malarial danger of the night, from the insects, from the hawk that could dive down on him at dawn and rip out an eye. She spread it over that immobile and cold body, taking care to turn it inside out, so that its color would be mixed with the color of the stones, moss, and grass around him. And she thought once again of the Holy Sepulchre, with a temporarily dead Christ who would soon be resurrected.

It was also her mother's first thought, as soon as she got up, to go see if the unfortunate man was dead or alive. He could be one or the other, since when she went to explore she found the place deserted. Not even the grass, which the dawn had lifted up like a sleeping child, kept a trace of him. All the better. She returned to her beloved coffee pot, to her dear hens, already announcing to the world that they had laid eggs. But now it was Conccezione who seemed to have fallen into a lethargic stupor, like a sleeping sickness. The sun was already high when her mother went to call her, but she answered with a piteous whine and went back to sleep.

It was the big day of the feast of Saint Cyril, Martyr. Since Serafino was occupied with the ceremonies in the cathedral, he couldn't come to the little church, so Giustina decided to take herself to town to hear mass. To tell the truth, she was also curious to see how things were going down there, to take a look at the vendors' benches, at the crowd of strangers, at the greased pole that had, attached to a circle of wood hanging off of its top, such delicacies as cheeses, salami, little packages, and bags of money, all for the one who climbed it first.

With the same pleasant expectation with which she took herself to the fair half a century ago, she dressed carefully, put on her good widow's shawl, and went out almost as though she were going to a secret appointment, closing Concezione and the cat inside the house. And the sleeper immediately felt that she was alone, with a mysterious sense of fear and anguish. She jumped out of bed and got dressed, ready to defend herself from any danger. But if there was ever a day of perfect quiet, this was it. Only one cloud, a cushion of white satin, leaned with sweet laziness against the highest peak of the mountain. Later, when the pealing of the bells wafted up from town, worn down by the haze of the hot day, the cloud moved, got larger, tore like a sack out of which came what looked like rags from a poor family of Gypsies that spread themselves throughout the bluish sky.

Concezione felt safer only when her mother came back in the door. As she had many years before, Giustina brought her a bar of torrone, and she began to gnaw on it with her strong Bedouin teeth. She was pleased when she heard that among the crowd, among so many hats and caps and berets and shawls, there was no flowered kerchief and visored cap of Comare Maria Giuseppa and her worthy nephew.

"But what did you do with the blanket, my soul?" asked her mother as she put her clothes back in the chest.

"I put it on the bottom because I didn't like to look at it."

"We should take out this cake before it gets moldy; besides, it's smeared honey all over the stuff and will attract ants."

Concezione took out the cake and took it to the little cupboard in the sacristy. Since the cupboard didn't close very well, flies and wasps got in and in their own way celebrated the feast of the holy martyr Cyril. In the hazy and now completely cloudy afternoon, Concezione was sweating because she had again wrapped the woolen kerchief around her head and chin to keep up the comedy of her toothache. Suddenly a bolt of lightning crossed the sky like a comet, with a great fiery tail. Not at once, but after seeming to have thought it over, an enormous roll of thunder shook the church and the rocks around it. Giustina ran to seek refuge at the feet of the little Madonna, followed by the frightened cat. But Concezione, as if a weight had suddenly been lifted, ran outside to collect on her face and her open hands the first big drops of rain. "Oh, this way those two won't come! Rain, rain, dear God—Glorious Saint Cyril, let loose more thunder and lightning, flood the road, send the archangels of heaven to keep the devils of the earth in place." And in fact there came down a torrent of water fragrant with a smell of earth, of stubble, of rocks, followed by a sly, never ending drizzle. This was the real feast for Concezione, because those two did not show up. Only the crooked acolyte came, with a dilapidated umbrella that looked like a bird with a hurt wing. He said that if the women wished it, Serafino would come the next day to celebrate mass, and announced that the fireworks had been postponed until the next evening and that the rain had hindered the race for the tree of goodies and the horse races, more important news for him and Giustina than the front page of a newspaper. And when Concezione gave him the cake to take to Serafino, he didn't hesitate to lick it all over, even if there was a wasp or two still stuck to it like to flypaper.

Comare Giustina and Signorino Costante came to mass the next day. It seemed to Concezione that Costante was all decked out with face powder—it must have been that joker of a barber who had brought him so low. But this time she had someone to protect and defend her: Serafino was there. When she served him his coffee in the sacristy, she said to him ardently, "That imbecile disgusts me and scares me; and that tarantula of his aunt does the same. Help me to get rid of them, Serafino. Only you can do it, and you will do it."

Under his fragile angelic shell, the little priest had a warrior's soul. He immediately understood Concezione's physical and moral terror and decided without doubt to confront her enemies. As long as he was in good company, in the women's kitchen, he was courteous and humble; in fact, he seemed almost intimidated by the giant presence of the youth, who for his part did nothing but show off his white and menacing teeth. But when he left, having understood that the other two, not having been invited to stay, needed to return to town, he waited for them on the road, walking slowly, with his breviary open between his hands, after having sent the malicious acolyte ahead.

He heard their footsteps on his trail, and had the impression that the imbecile had something bestial about him, between a satyr and a centaur. Concezione had to be saved.

The centaur walked ahead; he did not seem happy. He clenched his fists and kept showing his teeth in a grimace just like that of an unbroken horse straining at the bit. The woman instead stopped at the priest's side and looked with curiosity at the black book with the red edges that he had closed, keeping one finger inside to mark the interrupted page. She was curious and a bit disturbed, since the ancient superstitions of her village said that priests could use sacred books to remove spells, proclaim excommunications, curses, and misfortunes, heal the sick, exorcise those possessed by demons, enchant animals, keep temptation away; in short, that they had at the same time, if you like, a divine and an infernal power. To her, the little priest looked like a wax toy, with touches of color on his cheeks and hair just like a wax doll. Compared to the imbecile Costante, he seemed like one of those little men who are drawn next to the trunks of certain ancient trees to make their enormous size stand out better. He aroused in her a religious fear similar to the fear she felt for certain megalithic idols found in the rocky high plain of her country. Fabulous powers were attributed to them, for example, eating lightning bolts like spaghetti. Almost bewitched, she herself opened up the subject of Concezione.

"I love that child with all my soul; but she's odd, she seems almost under a spell. Your Lordship," and he didn't know whether she spoke seriously or in jest, "should use your books to take the spell off of her."

He tucked the breviary under his arm, almost to hide it from her sacrilegious eyes. Looking straight ahead, suddenly fierce, he said with a hard voice, "You should have respect for holy books; they are God's voice. Maria Concezione is a serious woman, even too wise for her age. It's true that she is not in good health, but her soul is healthy and vigorous."

"Oh, yes, and I love her more than I can tell you, more than a daughter. And I would like . . . "

"You are also a good woman, my dear, strong and generous. Maybe you are just a bit lacking in religion. What's more, you have certain fixations that aren't worthy of you: for example, pretending to love Concezione even as you want and plot for her an irreparable unhappiness."

"I? Why, Rector!"

"I am not a rector, and now I am speaking to you as a simple Christian: leave that poor creature in peace. She is doing her duty helping her mother; you might say she lives for her mother. And she does works of charity when she can. She doesn't ask anything else. Leave her in peace."

Her ruddy face paled. Tears of anger, humiliation, but also of tenderness veiled her eyes. She could not understand how she could want ill or unhappiness for Concezione, she who was ready to leave her all of her stuff, her house, even her bed. And she said as much. But, walking with slow brief steps, Serafino turned and looked her in the face.

"Very well," he said, "you can do just that when it's time; but don't think, don't even dream, that Concezione could sleep in your respectable bed with your nephew."

She gaped, showing her strong teeth almost like the imbecile did.

"But why not?"

"Is it possible, woman, that you don't understand? Above all because your nephew should never marry, not Maria Concezione nor any other woman on earth. He could only have degenerate children, maybe even worse than he is. And then too, because Concezione can't and doesn't want to, and maybe also shouldn't marry. She's sick; do you want to believe it or don't you? And her children would also be unfortunate."

"By this reasoning, no one in this world can get married. We all have some misfortune, more or less, and, sooner or later, we all have to die. Therefore . . . "

"Dear woman, you speak like a true aunt of your nephew."

At this, she became furious.

"You should rather say, my dear sir, that Concezione has a weakness: a weakness for no account men, not to say worse. We know the story of her youth, and let it go. When women are very young, they are all crazy. But now there's that other one: that stranger with the eyes of a cat, penniless and a whoremonger, excuse the word. He hangs around Concezione because he wants her money. He buzzes around like a wasp that pretends to be a butterfly. Just the day before yesterday he was seen wandering around by the church with a fife, dead drunk. Everyone knows it. They even told my Costante, since there are many wicked people in the world who like to torment innocent souls. It gnaws on my poor lad; he's jealous, and furious, even if he doesn't show it. If he happens to come upon that stranger, he will kill him like a flea."

The poor innocent, who had ears like a fox, also slowed his pace, clenched his fists, and began to shake. All of a sudden, he stopped, turned to Serafino, and with eyes red with anger, bringing a fist to his forehead, howled, "Either Maria, or pow!"

This time his aunt didn't laugh. Serafino grabbed Costante's other fist and held it between his hands like a hard apple. The imbecile tried in vain to free himself, but the little priest did not let go. Measuring himself against the giant, he said, "In the name of God, lad cast out this temptation!"

Overtaken by a shiver, the woman made the sign of the cross; it really was like casting off a spell, like an exorcism of one possessed by a demon. Costante dropped his other fist, he softened, his beautiful face was like that of a rebel angel pardoned by God.

They left that very morning, without returning to the house of the women. The fair had been a pretext for Costante and Concezione to get to know one another; but the aunt had to regret it, because when they passed the little church, he kept turning around, fascinated. And when they passed over into the valley, he hung his head on his chest and gave such a strong and insistent sob that Comare Maria Giuseppa wanted to pat him on the back like a choking child. For the moment, more than anything out of fear of Serafino and his occult powers, she decided to leave Concezione in peace. There was still time, and nobody ever knows what might happen in the future.

But fate had it that Concezione would not know peace so soon. And so, on the last night of the fair, while from the little wall of their garden she and her mother watched the far-off fireworks that embroidered the sky with comets, wheels of pearls, fabulous incandescent flowers, all the way up there in the hermitage of the two women, along with the rocket bursts, the cries of the crowd, and the crazy music of accordions, there arrived a man with a big hat that made a halo of his red, moon-lit face. He came up to the little gate and whistled.

"Oh," said Concezione, immediately alarmed, "it's Signor Bartoli, Aroldo's friend. He can't have come at this hour for his shirts. He seems tipsy too."

Her mother went to look, but did not open the gate, now closed with a chain and a rusty lock. In fact, the man stank of wine, but his eyes were good, blessed, wet with tenderness like two dewy periwinkles. His smile could only be compared to that of nurslings who suck and then let go of the maternal breast. But still the woman did not open. For some days now, she too had been afraid of everything. And then the break, at least so it seemed, with her old Comare Maria Giuseppa gave her a vague uneasiness, a premonition of some larger misfortune.

Bartoli demanded in a low and stammering voice, "Where is that blockhead?"

"Who?"

"Who else but Aroldo?"

"Who's seen him? It's months since we've seen him."

"Tch, tch," he said, strumming the poles of the gate like strings, "Tell me where he is. Is he inside?"

"You're crazy. I don't know why Signor Aroldo should be inside our house. Has he, perhaps, done something and needs to hide?"

"He's done this: he's the crazy one." He touched his fore-head, seemed angry, and then smiled again. "He hasn't been seen for three days. But, oh yes, I saw him coming this way. We had been drinking together, and he had his good guitar, and he said he wanted to give a serenade. 'Oh, go to hell,' I told him. 'You and your women,' since serenades are only for women. He headed in this direction; now, where is he?"

"I repeat: you're crazy. We've neither seen him nor heard him. And our house isn't a tavern that puts up drunks and their instruments."

Then Bartoli yelled with a voice like an angry rooster, "Signora Concezione, you are kindly requested to come here."

She approached, cautious and severe. She heard the man and asked him to lower his voice.

"Listen," she finally said with a certain displeasure, "if you think your companion is here, come look for him with the Carabinieri."

She pulled away her mother, who was shaking a bit, and made her go back into the house. And there, while Bartoli went away grumbling and staggering, they began to talk over the situation. A vague doubt, already tinged with fear, bothered both of them. If Aroldo had really not returned to the workers' encampment, nor to the hovel where he lived in town, he might have run into some ill treatment—let's put it that way for the moment—from the imbecile Costante or from the Giordanos. Everyone was mad at him. But how could he have hidden himself in some place and dropped out of sight? The mother said under her breath, as if to herself, "Have they killed him?"

"Oh no, Mamma, don't be silly. Let's not exaggerate. Anyway, what difference does it make?"

The mother started; she seemed to hear footsteps and noises in the garden. She wanted to go outside again, but Concezione held her back with a stubborn strength.

"Enough of these stories, Mamma. Now I'm tired of them. Really fed up. Why does everyone come to bother us? We don't go looking for anyone, don't bother anyone. Do we, or don't we have clean consciences? We do. So, be still and calm, Mamma. It will all pass." But she wasn't calm herself, and the sounds she really heard, the bursts of rockets and their echoes in the solitude, seemed to her gun shots from wild enemies intent only on hating and destroying them. She made her mother go to bed, and she settled herself to read her prayer book, populated with little holy cards which, more than the printed words, kept honest and holy company with her. She had some from her childhood: there was one from her first communion, with a nice fat cherub petting a white lamb among roses and daisies; and there was the last one, given to her by a nun in the hospital, with the deposition of Christ among a group of women who looked like sorrowful heroines of the theater. Christ, who had suffered so much, been humiliated, been forced to show his naked body to the inhuman crowd, had felt the gangrene pour out from his wounds onto his young, pure flesh, and had not complained, while we complain if a little thorn pricks us when we pick a rose.

She stayed up until the noises, far and near, were extinguished and only the song of the crickets floated up, with a silver flickering like dew on the grass. Then she also went to bed. She stretched out quietly next to her snoring mother, and in that quiet snoring, which didn't bother her since she had become accustomed to it over long years, she seemed to hear the murmuring of a mountain spring. Yes, her mother was calm, her conscience as pure as the spring water. And she also felt at peace with herself and others, at least about the events of those days. And, if pain and death were once again close to her, she offered them up in expiation for her past mistakes.

Three days went by. It was very hot, but still almost pleasant, like a steam bath where you sweat but aren't afraid to sweat because afterwards your skin is fresh and purified by the beneficent washing. Especially in the evening, after Giustina had watered the little clearing and the row of tomatoes that smelled like tropical plants, a truly religious peace like that of an ancient hermitage reigned around the little church. The setting moon was reminiscent of that at the feet of the little Madonna, and the constellations followed her on her journey like princesses in the train of a queen.

The two women were seated on the little bench. The old woman, her hand underneath her apron, counted her rosary beads, but Concezione didn't—she had no more desire to pray. It seemed to her that she had nothing more to ask, and that she no longer knew her prayers. It was enough to warm herself at her mother's side, as she had in those long ago nights of her infancy when that honest and protecting presence had been her whole world. What do we need to live? So little: a breath, a good word, the smell of the garden, the hope for the Kingdom of God that will surely come some day, even if with the peace of death, even without asking for it over and over again with careless words. She imagined this kingdom like a garden always fresh, always warm, without mosquitoes; a little bench against the wall illuminated by the moon, her mother's spirit next to hers, for eternity. She also tried to imagine the presence of her father, but she wasn't able to, nor the spirits of her more distant forebears, even if she forgave them all their presumed offenses. All of a sudden, though, it seemed that the desperate souls of her rogue ancestors returned to earth to disturb the peace of the two innocent women. It was a torrid morning, hazy, the sky veiled as if with medicinal gauze. Hellish puffs of the scirocco* carried dust and remnants of burnt stubble into the clearing of the house. To save herself from this dirt, Giustina closed the door and then went to help Concezione remake the big bed. All of a sudden they heard a knocking, discreet but insistent taps, until Concezione, alarmed, went to open. Her eyes widened when she saw the impressive personage there. He had on a dark uniform with red stripes, a matching hat with a visor. His face was pleasing, almost handsome: plump, rosy, and fresh, but cut in two by a large black mustache like the tails of two irritated black cats; it seemed to be stuck under his short nose to frighten people. His large black eyes, deliberately frowning, increased this impression. Noting the inevitable effect on Concezione's pale face, he grimaced, but just to hide a mocking smile. He introduced himself in a cadenced voice that also seemed mocking.

"I am the sergeant of the Carabinieri. I need some information."

She was uncertain whether or not to invite him in; then her mother, who understood immediately what was going on, came over and spoke respectfully.

---

*Scirocco: the hot wind that blows across the Mediterranean from the southwest, out of Africa.

"Please come in, Your Lordship, sit down. Forgive our poor place."

"Here then," he said, coming in but neither sitting down nor paying any attention to the poverty of the place. "I am looking for information about a certain Aroldo Aroldi, a laborer on the road project."

Concezione impulsively protested, "What do we know?"

Her mother, instead, with a troubled heart, yet strong in her clean conscience, asked, "May we know why?"

"The young man has been missing for six days, and he was last seen heading in this direction."

"It's true," said the determined mother, "that we also saw him six days ago, sitting on a boulder here above the mountain road. He was drunk. I went to tell him that he wasn't safe there, that he could fall asleep and get his wallet stolen. He answered me rudely, but I still helped him to get down and stretch out in the shade. We didn't see him after that, nor have we heard anything about him."

Concezione stayed quiet. Nevertheless, the man of law looked in her direction, and went on in the strange guttural melody of his calm voice.

"Had he, the young man, known you for a long time? And for what reason?"

Concezione replied fiercely, "I work on men's clothing. All the bachelors in town, especially those without a family, come to me. They bring me the material; I take measurements and make the clothes."

The sergeant, a bachelor without family, was personally pleasantly struck by this news, all the more because Concezione's eyes, limpid and serious in spite of their pride, or rather because of it, gazed at him almost defiantly; and when she spoke he saw all her clean, white teeth like those of a fifteen-year-old girl.

"Ah, you sew? By hand or by machine?"

"By hand, by hand. The clothes come out better and never tear."

"So then, this young man, this Aroldi, came here for that reason?"

"Exactly," Concezione confirmed, while, trembling, her mother admired the cleverness of the functionary. "He came about a year ago, when they were beginning the road work. He also wanted to room with us, but we don't have room, and we are solitary women. He came back a number of times, up until a few months ago. After that we didn't hear anything more from him."

But the sergeant knew more.

"Someone has said, Signorina, that you and Aroldi were engaged."

"I won't deny," said Concezione decisively, flattered by that serious "Signorina," "I won't deny that Signor Aroldi courted me a bit; but I didn't pay any attention to him, not to him nor to others."

She immediately regretted this useless addition, all the more because the sergeant arched his thick brows, and, even if he did not carry it off to perfection, he pretended to be grim, sure of himself. Looking at Concezione, it didn't even occur to him that she might be guilty or even responsible for the disappearance of Aroldo; but she must know something about what happened and he must make her talk at all costs, for the prestige of the "Meritorious Corps."[*]

He began to throw out small inaccuracies.

"We have precise information contrary to what you are saying. We've heard that Signor Aroldi has always frequented these premises; that he came also at night, and that you . . . "

"It's not true! Your informers are for the most part unscrupulous people interested in gossip."

"Give me a few names."

"No, I'm not naming any names; you know them better than I do."

"Signorina!" he exclaimed severely, to remind her of the order and respect due to himself. But Concezione had already understood who she was dealing with, and wanted to

---

[*] *L'arma benemerita:* the Corps of Carabinieri.

defend herself, and even vindicate herself from all those who bothered her.

"Yes, sir, there are people who enjoy bothering even poor women like ourselves. My mother and I live as though we were already in our tombs, far from the world, without asking anything from any living soul, and even so we are not left in peace. Get it well in your mind, Signor Sergeant, that neither my mother nor I know anything about the events for which you have taken the trouble to come here. That's the truth. The rest is in the hands of God."

"You forget, Signorina, that I can also take you into custody."

She started to laugh. Stretching out her long, pale, hands she said calmly, "Then put the handcuffs on me—do you have them with you?"

His face also lightened with amusement, and then the mother decided to intervene again.

"Do you know what happened? That boy always said he wanted to go seek his fortune in America. He even said he already had some sort of good offer. He must have left without telling anyone."

But the man shook his head because the report of Aroldo's disappearance had come in fact from the road construction company, and the missing man had neither money nor a passport. Furthermore, he was very diligent in his work, scrupulous about his contract with the manager, faithful to his companions, loyal and sincere.

In spite of his almost insolent tone of voice, Concezione felt her heart swell. She thought about the subterranean passage, perhaps known by some low life, and in which, perhaps, some horrible new mystery was enclosed. But at the same time, at least for the moment, she needed to keep her secret suspicion locked up in her soul, partly in memory of her ancestors.

The sergeant went on, "Out in the world everything becomes known, Signorina; the air itself spies and carries things around. Therefore, we know that you and Signor Aroldi were almost, let's put it this way, engaged to be married. Then one fine day, a bad day for him, the project came to nothing. Then people saw that Aroldi's mode of life changed: he went to women, he went to the tavern, now we don't exactly know where he went. And we need to know, as soon as possible. So don't you make those dove eyes at me; you know something, and it's your duty to tell the law."

She crossed her arms and touched her breast. She thought that the first judge of every human action is God. So she made an instant examination of conscience, found herself innocent, and had no wish to accuse anyone.

"I swear to you as if I were in a courtroom that I can't give you any precise information, Sergeant."

"But you do have suspicions."

"If I have them I'll keep them to myself. I can't accuse any living soul; I don't know a thing about what might have happened. I couldn't say more even if you put me over the fire."

Then he turned to the mother, but by now she also knew what line to take, and he wasn't able to get one word more from her than what Concezione had already said.

Still, they were both dismayed when the sergeant asked them to accompany him to the place where they had seen Aroldo in a drunken sleep, and they followed him reluctantly.

The wind blew hard and lifted up Concezione's skirt. She noticed that as he looked at her legs, the sergeant let it be seen that he was also a man of the world like all the others. Bending over to gather her clothing to herself, after having tied under her chin the kerchief that in such cases still served as a half mask and refuge, she drew near her mother and touched her skirt to warn her to be careful. Cautiously, the woman went along the path, among the stones and the rocks where the moss, shivering in the wind, had the texture of felt. There was no trace of the missing man. They could only see what looked like black berries in the grass, to be avoided because they were the sign that a flock of goats had passed by.

A bit heavily, but undaunted, the sergeant clambered up on the boulder where Giustina said she had seen Aroldo. He explored the area with eyes like binoculars, as he defended his winglike mustache from the impertinent puffs of the scirocco. Nothing: the mountain, the valleys, the church, the roads, the black jagged profile of the town, all immersed in the wind, said nothing, neither about his fantasy nor about the purpose for which he was going to so much trouble.

Deep down, if it had not been for the prestige of the "Meritorious Corps," and for his duty, he would not have cared much about the missing man. But with his raw instinct of a man of law and order, he felt that Concezione was mocking him, and he wanted to win.

He climbed down, felt the rock, bent over to look at the ground, and finally discovered something. Like a thread of revealing blood, a piece of red string clung to a stalk of wild oats. It was thinner than a thread of a spider's web, but as powerful as a rope to cling to in an emergency. He picked it up, stretched it out delicately between the thumb and index finger between one hand and the other like a hair, and put it under Concezione's eyes. She didn't bat an eyelash, but inside her closed mouth she felt her teeth chatter. Yes, it was a thread from the famous blanket, but, after all, what difference did it make? She had done an act of charity to cover up the drunkard, why should she shake? But still, she was shaking. She felt that Aroldo must have hurt himself, *like that other one*, and that ancient remorse attached itself to this one.

"Those are threads that the birds carry around," said the mother, convinced. And the capable Signor Calogero put the thread in his wallet, thinking that this simple thread could guide him a long way.

Later on, Pietro Giordano arrived. Now that the post was vacant, or at least gave the macabre appearance of being vacant, he could try again. The fact was that he had fallen deeply in love with Concezione, that witch with the eyes of a fairy. And if he counted on her ten thousand scudi, he counted on them in a noble way, that is, for the well-being of their future family.

They became magically changed into pigs, cows, sheep, those ten thousand scudi; and he saw them walking, grazing, mating, and multiplying evangelically.

He sat on a stump in the clearing and began by telling a lie. He said that Serafino had sent him to find out whether there was any truth in the recent gossip about the disappearance of Aroldo.

Irritated, Concezione snapped back. What did she know and what did it matter to her? Maybe Pietro himself was better informed. And he knit his ferocious brows.

"What do you mean to say? That I killed him?"

"Anything is possible."

He bent over until his hands grabbed his feet. A growl like that of a beaten dog came out of his panting breast. She was frightened. Oh, how these bestial men came to hunt her, leaving her like a doe targeted in her lair!

"Pietro, I didn't mean to offend you. I was joking."

"You don't joke about these things, woman! One word is enough to light a destructive fire. Not only that, but I tell you that, if you want, if you ask me to, I can be of use to you in this ugly story, that is, to flush out the truth."

She had an impulse, a desire to take him up on it, but she repressed it at once. The ugly story, she said, interested her only to a certain point: it was up to those in charge to discover the truth. And besides, she thought the stranger had disappeared of his own free will, happy man, just to get out from under the gossip and bother of this damned town. Pietro agreed with her.

"That's absolutely true as far as it's concerned. I'm happy when I am with my cows; they love me and don't chatter, and mind their own business. I wouldn't ever go back to town, because every time they fill my heart with rubble and spines."

"So then, why have you come?"

"Above all for my own business, and I swear to you that I didn't know anything about the business of the stranger. But immediately they began to poke at me, to tell me that you were almost happy to be free of him. And so I thought . . . "

She grabbed a stone and threw it at him; it hit him in the knee. He felt pain, but beatifically. He bent over again, picked up the stone and held it in his fist like a precious object.

"You're right," he said, "You didn't have any attachment to him. You aren't tied to anyone, and that's good. But tell me, beauty, what will you do when you get old?"

"What all old women do, handsome. I'll dunk my bread, I'll pray, I'll wait for death. But I won't live to be an old woman," she added, as if talking to herself. "I'll die young, and maybe in not too many years."

"Bah! Now you want to make me cry. And who will you leave your money to?"

"That's my own business; besides, I don't have money—it's your grandfather who has spread that nonsense."

"All the better," said Pietro, his eyes aflame. "That way, if I tell you I'm crazy about you, really crazy, you know, cooked like a pear in the oven, then you'll believe me. My brother Paolo also calls out for you in his sleep, but I have spoken to him clearly: 'Brother, I love you like my own eyes, but in this case we need to understand one another. I am the firstborn, and if you don't get it from words, you'll get it from my punches.' In fact, he started to growl, so I gave him a shower of punches to make him understand once and for all that we are not Siamese twins, who go to bed together with one woman. Now he's sulking, but I couldn't care less, and that's why I have come here by myself."

"I'm sorry, Pietro, that there are problems between you on my behalf. But, I repeat, you're like those shepherds who fought over the stars—do you know the story? Those two able youths were lying belly-up on a beautiful starry night. One said, 'I would like to have a meadow as big as the sky.' And the other said, 'And I want as many sheep as the stars I see.' 'And where will you pasture them?' asked the other. 'In your meadow.' 'But I don't plan to give you permission.' And so they came to words and then to blows."

But Pietro didn't feel like laughing.

"And yet, you will give up, Maria Concezione, I assure you that you will give up. Because I am young, strong, and stubborn. When I get something in my head, there isn't a blessed soul who can take it from me. I'll court you for twenty or thirty years, and you will give up."

"To your health!" she laughed, truly flattered and entertained, "Just don't be a nuisance."

"We'll see about that," he said, getting up from the stump and giving it a kick. He had become surly, enflamed with the desire to assault her, kiss her, bite her face; but she defended herself with feminine astuteness.

"Watch yourself, boy. Don't do anything foolish, or else they'll blame you for the stranger's disappearance."

Pietro gave a little start, and Concezione suspected him too.

The shadow of the missing man grew larger and darker every day, like the shadows that lengthen at sunset. A commissioner of public safety came in person and interrogated the two women with the same results as the sergeant. They made a site visit to the place where Aroldo had been seen the last time. He threatened Concezione with arrest. Then once again, silence.

The summer followed its slow and suffocating course. It hadn't rained in a long time, and the well of the two women was almost dry. The mother walked kilometers every day to get water, and Concezione would have been afraid to be alone, did not some harmless person continually show up to keep her company.

The old phlebotomist had also become a regular visitor, but he never stopped talking about the missing man, and never without a certain irony. He seemed to find the strange happenings very entertaining, and anyway, all the other idlers were talking about it. Women kept their children locked up at home for fear that they would be stolen. Calmer people, though, were convinced that the stranger, provided with a passport in some way that would become known, and perhaps also with money, had gone off on his own business.

The "doctor" exasperated Concezione. Sometimes he even managed to mesmerize and frighten her, weaving his own special version of the mysterious happenings.

"It probably happened like this: that simpleton was practically out of his head with passion for you, and even more from the sucking of that vampire, the lovely Maria Pasqua. Everyone knows what type of bat that one is: a mammalian bird, the devil's spore. She likes money, handsome young men, and no children, neither sons nor daughters. I think she also likes wine, and *rosolio*. She's like certain vampires in America that, during the hot season, land on the necks of overheated horses and make a breeze with their wings so that their victims feel somewhat refreshed and happily let them suck their blood; that's what that Siren does with her lovers. She drank the blood of Aroldo—a nice name, like a troubadour, and he even has a mandolin—and when the blond boy tried to console himself, other than with music, wine, and *acquavita*, he fell lower and lower. When he was drunk, he talked about his suffering over you—oh yes, you, Signora Maria Concezione—and some people laughed at him. Others listened to him seriously, and trailed him; and these, probably, have made him vanish like a cloud at sunset."

"But who, who, for the love of God? You tell me, Doctor; you act like those American vampires with me."

"Maybe so! You really would restore my blood, if you let me suck your sweet neck. Because you, my friend, have hot blood, boiling, even if you pretend otherwise. Happy the man who will succeed in sucking even one drop from your lips!"

And he stretched out his trembling hand, with veins like the leeches he once applied to the sick; but Concezione was quick to move away with indescribable repugnance. She was more afraid of him than of all her other suitors put together. Even so, like children on the sad evenings of winter, she shivered with a pleasant anguish when he began again to tell stories about the subterranean passage, and concluded, if jokingly, that

Aroldo too had been lured in there and maybe was still in there, with his guitar, like a bird in a cage.

Then she protested, still painfully repeating her futile question, "But who? Who could it have been?"

"You know better than I do, fickle girl."

"Stop joking, Doctor. Do me a favor: go away, and don't talk like that anywhere else."

He pretended to obey: he bowed, and went away with dignity, leaving her in great agitation. She thought she was going mad. Aroldo's image was always before her, alive, touchable, with beautiful, sad eyes, and lips held out to kiss. And now that he wasn't there anymore, and would never be there again, she felt she loved him, wanted him, with all her truly incandescent blood. Not only that, but it seemed to her that now her only reason for living was no longer her affection for her mother, but this love for him.

"If he were to reappear! If he were to come back! I would give myself to him without thinking about anything else. I would cling to him until I became one body with his—like that, like that!"

And she bit her lips with a spasm. She threw herself on the bed crying, embraced by the shadow of nothingness.

On a moonlit night, the sergeant came back. He immediately said, in his voice like a bubbling fountain, "Don't be afraid, Signorina. I just stopped by because I was going by here on some business."

It's true that such personages have business in all the most remote corners of the world, wherever the devil tries to hide with all his malevolent inventions. But then, in the neighborhood of the little church protected by the little Madonna, since the death of those ancestors, evil had little hold; even Aroldo's case could not yet be clearly judged. At any rate, Concezione had secretly prided herself on being more clever than the sergeant, and she put herself on the alert But she was courteous, even to the point of asking if he would like a cup of coffee.

"It would be very welcome; even more so if it were prepared with your beautiful hands."

Concezione's hands were not beautiful, at least not in the common sense of the word. But they were full of expression, light brown, pale, nervous, with short clean nails naturally rosy and shiny. She looked at them; she seemed to smile at them, and her hands responded that the man was there for her.

She was alone in the house once more, since her mother had gone in search of water. She put the coffeepot on the fire and prepared the tray.

He followed her calm movements with a soft gaze of almost paternal tenderness. He had learned many things in those days of investigation, among other things about the money deposited in the bank; and Concezione looked good with a lightly gilded halo around her head, like a Coptic Madonna. But he also wanted to be clever; gallant, yes, but clever.

"Very kind, very kind, Signorina. This is excellent coffee; this is the first exquisite coffee I have had in this town."

"Have you been here long?" she asked, sitting down in front of him, but at a respectful distance.

"About six months. And, to tell you the truth, I like it a lot. It's not, after all, the den of scoundrels, not to say worse, that they had painted for me. Maybe," he added, between vanity and mockery, "to flatter me into coming here. They are, rather, respectable people, tranquil, hard working. The worst are those little villages on the outskirts, especially those in the mountains. The thin air, let's admit it, stimulates fantasies, and our good mountaineers are not always disposed to fantasizing chivalrous enterprises. They fight among themselves, and when they can, they come down into the valley in search of adventure. But you, Signorina, probably know them better than I do. I was up there the other day." With his spoon, he indicated a vague point, far away through the window. "And I met some pretty types; among others, Signora Maria Giuseppa Alivia. In fact, she told me that she is a good friend of yours and of Signora Giustina."

"Ah," said Concezione with distracted surprise, then seemed to catch herself. "Ah, yes, we know her. She's really an eccentric type, but good, generous, open hearted."

"She herself invited me to her house, through a mutual friend. And with the vanity that belongs to rich, rough peasants, she made me see all of her castle and the treasures it holds, also the provisions, also the stuff in the chests. It was entertaining, I won't deny it. Signora Maria Giuseppa has at least a hundred sets of sheets, and a good fifty bed blankets, perhaps woven back in the days when Berta spun.* Indeed, she informed me that she had given one of these blankets to you, Signorina Concezione, as a good omen of the impending marriage." (Concezione, in spite of all her religion, swore within herself against that mad horse of a Comare Maria Giuseppa.) "Her husband was there too, Mr. Battistino Alivia, a good-natured man who spat, chuckled, drank, offered drink, and then spat again. His wife says he doesn't open his mouth for anything else. And yet, when I sat down next to him, he asked me point-blank, 'What happened in the case of that stranger who disappeared? Are they blackmailing him, by any chance?' You understand, Signorina, that I couldn't say anything, but Signora Alivia broke in and said something big. She said that the stranger was certainly made to disappear by some suitor of Maria Concezione."

"Whose?"

"Yours, Signorina."

"Mine?" she cried, and she rolled her eyes which looked like those of a trampled serpent. And truly enraged, tired of all of those malevolent and villainous allusions, she said, "For that matter, Costante Alivia, the imbecile nephew of Signora Maria Giuseppa, is also one of my suitors."

She immediately regretted it, but it was too late. The sergeant had put his cup down on the table next to him. Then he stuck a hand in his pocket, and with his large fingers with

---

Fin dal tempo in cui Berta filava: a folk expression meaning "a long time ago."

sensitive fingertips, he stroked a paper envelope, in which there
was the thread found in the grass where Aroldo had slept off
his intoxication. That thread, even so well wrapped up, gave
him an almost electric shock, because he had observed that its
color and texture corresponded almost perfectly to those of
some blankets of Signora Maria Giuseppa; and, as a man of the
law, but also as a sensual and cunning man, he reconstructed
in his own way the events of that famous night. Aroldo had an
appointment with Concezione; she went there, she lay down
on the grass with her young lover, and for various reasons of
decency she had brought with her the almost nuptial blanket.
This fantasy excited him, awakened other fantasies, made him
almost happy.

"Ah," he said, kindly and craftily, "Signor Costante, too!
So then, how many suitors do you have? Let's see now."

But Concezione showed her teeth in a snarl, just like she
had seen the imbecile do.

"Yes," she said, "and then throw them all in jail for me."

He started again to tell the story of his trip to the little
mountain village, but naturally without saying that it was in fact
because anonymous accusations had given him to understand
that Costante the imbecile, who was, notwithstanding the surveillance of his aunt, drunk like all the rest during the days of
the fair, had made death threats against the stranger who wanted
to take Concezione away from him. So the whole thing, the
trip to the village, the meeting with the friend he had in common with the Alivias, the visit to their house, had all been
arranged and set out in advance; and it seemed to him it had
also turned out well.

"They are a curious and primitive people in that little
village. In one house I saw a sort of cradle made out of the
bark of a cork tree, tied to a rafter with four ropes, and in this
hammock made by savages there was a beautiful baby. 'It's to
protect him from the rats, the vampires, and the pig,' said his
mother, as she ground roasted acorns to make coffee. And the
church? Absolutely crumbling, even though the old people go
there to pray anyway; but Signora Alivia, who spends thousands

of lire on disputes over a few centimeters of land doesn't think to restore the altar."

Noting Concezione's cold but attentive silence, he continued, "I also met your gallant suitor, this Signorino Costante, who does nothing all day long but lean a shoulder against the wall of the tavern. Not knowing what else to do, he plays *morra* with his shadow. But he's a handsome boy, a hunk of boy who looks like a bull. You should marry him, Signorina; you could do a lot of good to that miserable place."

Concezione looked at him, as troubled and cold as trampled snow. Now she had understood everything, and her cleverness was gone, replaced by a profound anguish. Oh no, she didn't want to hurt anyone. Even if the imbecile's guilt was indisputable, she wouldn't have added a syllable to make matters worse. But she couldn't defend him either, so she remained silent. The arrival of her mother, with a large jug on her head and a small one in each hand, brought her a double relief. She took the jar off her head with both of her burning hands, put it on the little bench, and bent over to drink as if from a fountain. Then, while Giustina went to lower the two little jars into the well with ropes tied to their handles so that the water would stay cool, she went back to sit down in front of the sergeant. Almost without hearing anything else he said, she waited patiently for him to finish and be gone.

They came, they went, they stopped to see the two women—men, old people, boys, peasants, townspeople. And they all broached the question of the missing stranger. The place had never been so crowded. The clearing of the little church became the midpoint of the evening strolls of all the idlers of the town in those long summer twilights when a breath of fresh air came down from the mountains, and the glowing of the horizons open to the ends of the valley gave the illusion of the sea. Some sat on the little wall around the clearing; others continued into the surrounding area. And then they went to see where he had been swallowed up by the ground, or kidnapped by some ogre of the mountain grottos, that young stranger whose image had begun to take on a legendary hue, and thus become one with the others in that painting that had as a background the primitive landscape and the granite Sphinxes of the huge rocks.

Sometimes Giustina went outside to take part in the conversations, but without ever losing her prudence and the measure of her words. Concezione instead hid with her work behind the shed, even if people entered the garden or the house, and waited for them all to leave. It seemed to her that they would have had more solitude in a crowded house in the city than in this place, ironically called "of solitude."

She hadn't had any more visits from the sergeant, but she heard that he hadn't given up, that he continued his investigations, and this didn't displease her. She also wanted to know the truth, even if it were a cruel truth. That was the only way she would be able to calm herself and take her old life up again. She made a vow to the Madonna: "If he comes back, if he is alive and safe, I'll spend half of my money to decorate the church."

In the meantime, she would have liked to have spent it to do her own research, but she didn't dare talk about it with anyone. She didn't trust anybody. When her mother was absent, she slipped furtively into the little church. She tried the bricks one by one, she tapped on the pavement, she dug holes which she was then careful to close with cement, and got up sweating and panting, squeezing her head between her hands.

"I'm crazy, I know it; I'm crazy," she moaned out loud, but she didn't stop her futile searches.

She would have liked to have at least confided in Serafino, under the seal of the confession, but he, too, he more than anyone else, awakened in her distrust and almost repugnance. She saw him for the first time in his true guise of a weak man, sick, fanatic. What help could he give her? And when she realized that this desperation of hers cut into her religious faith she felt that a cold, hard terror, like some supernatural danger, more frightening than her illness, menaced her. In those bright nights of late summer, she dreamed that two moons were pursuing one another in heaven. They came to blows, they broke into pieces, the earth became filled with pieces of yellow gold on which it was no longer possible to walk, and people died of hunger and of thirst. Nature really did turn the color of gold. The leaves fell off the fig tree, fleshy and shriveled like hands tired of fighting. The leaves fell off the willow and ran through the grass like lizards glowing in the sun. Those of the grape vine lit up like flames, and the clusters of grapes were assailed by the wasps, who were also gold. Evenings began to be cool, and people didn't come out walking as far as the little church anymore. All the better. Concezione now preferred winter to summer. In the winter, desires grow fainter, the senses are soothed like the earth in repose; the company of the living fire calls to mind the company of the dear departed. And by this point the memory of the blond stranger was confused with that of the brown boy. Maybe their spirits ran together, with the clouds, on the peaks of the mountains, playing like children in the garden of eternity. In this way, a bit of a visionary, she confused earth with heaven. And sometimes she liked to imagine that those two spirits, the spirits of those two who, alive, had known the taste of her mouth, were close to her, talking about their schemes. One recounted the projects he had carried out, a trip to set up a distant city, the other calmly told the story of how he had managed to hang himself.

Concezione didn't cast them out; spirits can't be cast out. But once in awhile, in her lucid and innocuous hallucinations, it seemed that those two ended up arguing. Aroldo, the meek one, accused the violent one of having ruined Concezione with his arrogance, his sensuality, the offense against human and divine laws; and the other retorted, "And you ruined her worse than I did by being a sissy."

She shook herself, trying to laugh at herself and her foolish fancies, because, down deep, she had a certain human sense of waiting, of change of situation, of a fact, in short, that ought to stir up that chilly, swampy calm in which she stagnated. It was that instinct of waiting that old people and ill people also have, and she thought in vain that if her own life had to change, it could only change for the worse. Hope glowed in the depths of her heart, like a jewel, even if stolen and hidden in the bottom of a well.

And then one day Comare Maria Giuseppa arrived with a face as dark and grim as a winter's day. She hadn't forgotten to fill her knapsack, but this time she didn't empty it in the house of her hostesses, nor did she even bring her horse into the frosty garden, but left it outside the gate almost as if to be able to leave again immediately. She must have some big case to discuss in the magistrate's court or in the court of justice, some mix-up that was cloudier and more complicated than the others.

"Yes," she said arrogantly, lifting her spurred leg like an irritated rooster, "you've fixed me but good. That miserable idiot, that animal of my nephew Costante, has been arrested on the charge of having killed and hidden the stranger."

Concezione retorted, quick and contemptuous, "What do we have to do with that?"

"Damn my soul, and what do you have to do with it, if the stranger hung around these parts because of your eyes? You were the one who flattered and attracted him."

In her conscience, Concezione knew that it was so, but she couldn't confess it. She became livid and said, "For once, watch your tongue. You can only hurt your nephew, if indeed it's possible to hurt him more than God already has. And as for my actions, did I come to tell you about them? Have I ever been intimate with you or listened to you?"

"That's it, exactly, damn my soul. If you had behaved like a wise woman," ("Look who's talking," said Concezione to herself) "if you had listened to my advice, things wouldn't have happened this way. We would all be happy now, instead of between the claws of the law and the devil."

She made the sign of the cross, either against earthly justice or the devil, but Comare Giustina interrupted, calm and not much alarmed.

"All right then, sit down and at least have a cup of coffee. Everything can be fixed with time and money. So tell us what happened."

"It happened like this: as soon as he saw her, my nephew fell in love with Concezione, madly, foolishly in love." ("And how else could he have done it?" thought Concezione.) "Anyway, you heard him; all he could do was repeat 'Either Maria, or I'll shoot myself.' And then that priest, that little priest of spittle" (now that he and his book were far away, she could allow herself to talk like this) "calmed him down. It was like he freed him from temptation. But then that idiot Costante got another obsession: when he heard the story about the stranger, he got it in his head, and bragged about it to everyone, that he himself had killed him and hidden him. And so in the end they arrested him. Now he's in jail, and I have to find him a damned lawyer."

"But what's the truth?"

"The truth is that he is as innocent as the donkey he is. But now I have to work and spend, lose sleep and my health."

Concezione was on the point of saying "It serves you right," but reassured by the peevish, not sorrowful, tones of the woman who, deep down, perhaps would enjoy dealing with lawyers and judges, she thought that the imbecile must certainly be innocent, and that things would soon be smoothed out. But then she rebelled at Comare Maria Giuseppa's demand that she, Concezione in person, accompany her to the lawyer to affirm Costante's innocence.

"You're crazy. I don't know anything, and I have had enough annoyance about this business."

"Then I'll bring the lawyer here to you. You must absolutely speak to him. You have to save one who is in danger of death for your sake. You are the cause of all of this, and you shouldn't shirk your responsibility."

This was Comare Maria Giuseppa's logic. She trotted out the articles of the penal code against the insidious instigators of crimes, about reticent testimony, about tacit encouragement of evil doing. And after insistence, threats, and pounding on the table, she went away stamping her feet and promising to return with a lawyer and, if needed, with ready witnesses. It would all have been laughable, had Concezione at least had someone to defend her; but she felt alone, bewildered, the prey of a truly diabolical fate.

The only thing she could do was hide, and a subterranean passage would now have been very useful to her. Driven by a sort of mania, in spite of the reassurances and comforting words of her mother, she slipped out of the garden and went towards the mountain path, headed towards the point where Aroldo had disappeared. She was guided by a type of morbid instinct of criminals who return to the scene of the crime.

The grass grew thick, almost black, in the shade of the rocks, and the moss on the rocks also took on the color of winter vegetation, a brownish yellow type of green. The moss was high, thick, as if the stones had covered themselves with thicker fur to resist the cold.

The sun was tepid, but the air was cold, with a crystalline stiffness. The crows had made their first appearance, announcing with their croaking not only the bad season, but something unspeakably sad. They seemed to have come from a land of everlasting ice, eternal nights, and to have brought with them, scattering like the seeds of death, a funereal desperation. And also up above, in certain ravines of the mountain, in spite of the clear day, the beginning of a fog rose like smoke; up there too, the spirits of solitude had already lit their winter fires.

Concezione felt her feet grow damp, but she continued to climb. Here is the place where Aroldo was seated, with his guitar, his love, and his drunkenness. From up there you could see the whole road that led to the town, and the profile of the town facing the valley, with the towers of the cathedral and the prison, the remains of an old fortress, almost resembling one another. She thought she could see, in the courtyard of the prison, the imbecile Costante, blissful about the crime he believed he had committed. And she was angry; but just at that moment, she felt that her first duty was not to flee and escape from all this painful mess, but rather to help the innocent and save the weak. The panorama of her conscience suddenly seemed to her different from the ordinary, like that of the valleys and towns seen from up high: sad, yes, echoing with sinister voices, but clear and transparent in its hardness.

She should do her duty, say what she knew about the truth, take on her part of the responsibility. She went back down, therefore, took up her work again, and with a still heart waited for what would happen. But Comare Maria Giuseppa returned by herself, with her knapsack empty, her face fallen. The lawyer had received her almost mockingly, advising her to leave Concezione in peace and not to gossip.

"But I have an idea," she whispered. "There's that yellowish little priest, who resembles a little tame fox, who has shown he has an almost magical power over Costante. Couldn't he be sent to talk to him in prison, to convince him not to say any more nonsense, not to claim that he's guilty, in short, to put himself back on the road to salvation? They didn't allow me to see the boy today; but if the priest says he wants to hear his confession, they'll let him in for sure. I'll give him a present: I'll send him three pounds of honey and two fresh cheeses."

Without stopping her work, Concezione said, "Why don't you go tell him yourself?"

"Because I think you have more power over him. He's also in love with you, and you can trust him."

Despite Comare Maria Giuseppa's new inductions, Concezione thought that maybe Serafino really could do something for the imbecile. But was the imbecile really innocent after all? She didn't know; she was no longer sure of anything. At any rate, she quickly put aside the idea of turning to Serafino because the little acolyte arrived with bad news about him. The little priest had to take to his bed because the first cold weather, and the religious labors from which he never excused himself—getting up at dawn for mass, teaching catechism to children and women—had reopened the holes in his lungs. He had vomited blood, and now he lay exhausted on his little bed of a virgin martyr, tormented more by the inability to continue his works of charity than by his illness.

Concezione felt herself taken up again in that circle of pain and death. What could she do? She started praying again, "Lord, Thy will be done;" and she fell again into a mode of waiting, as if she had fallen to the bottom of a ravine and was waiting, even with broken bones, for superhuman help.

A thread of hope came from the very quarter from which she least expected it: from Signor Calogero. He came towards evening, when it was already dark, and he was dressed in civilian clothes, with a blue tie and starched white cuffs that came down to the middle of his hands. His eyes shone in his flushed face; he looked like a country merchant dressed for the fair, hoping for excellent business. Concezione felt a certain sympathy for him, that sympathy that all true gentlemen inspire in honest folk. She felt he was a good man, simple, cordial, even without being able to explain why he had chosen that thankless profession of his. But then she thought that a man of justice needed exactly the virtues of Signor Calogero, and she trusted him.

He began with the usual simple-minded lie that he just happened to be passing that way and had come in to find out if Concezione had heard anything about Aroldo. That way, in private, among friends, she could speak in confidence. But she widened her eyes and felt her heart beat.

"What do you mean, news? Didn't I hear they arrested Costante the imbecile on the charge that he killed and hid the stranger?"

"That doesn't mean anything. Idiots have always been like that, since the creation of the world. Wasn't Adam himself an idiot? And if Signor Costante wants to make himself out a hero to look good for you, Signorina, what can you do?"

She shook her head, serious. He continued, lowering his voice, "Anyway, he's not the only one around here who is simple minded, a visionary. Believe me, there are others. It's a disease that spreads in solitary places, where everything seems quiet, but there's really a worse hubbub than in inhabited areas. Well then, there's another of your admirers, Signorina, one, it would seem, with his wits about him much more than the imbecile, who says he's seen Signorino Aroldo up in the woods on the mountain. He goes about emaciated and in rags, like a hunted animal, and sleeps in caves, and eats what the pig herders give him as charity."

"But is everybody crazy?" she cried, and she felt like she had also caught the mysterious mental illness the sergeant had mentioned. But down deep she felt a sense of relief: Aroldo alive! Maybe also out of his mind; but they could catch him like a hare, and take him to the mad house. That would be better than if he had died a bad death and been buried in unconsecrated ground.

The sergeant smiled, with two happy furrows around his mouth. He did not grow tired of looking at her, almost enjoying her there in front of him so bewildered and anxious, happy to simultaneously torment her and console her.

Counting off the fingers of his left hand with his right index finger, he said, "Yes, all crazy. Crazy because of you. Do you want to count them as five or as six?"

And he named the Giordanos, the imbecile, Aroldo, the doctor, and finally, bursting into laughter, Signor Calogero.

"Oh, go on," said Concezione, herself overcome by an unexpected merriment. "You are a great big joker; you make me wonder how they ever put you in that position."

Then he heaved himself up, proud, austere, puffing out his chest so that it seemed padded. His mustaches stuck out straight like those of an angry cat. His bubbling voice sounded like that of a creek.

"Nobody in the world knows how to be in his position the way I do in mine. And you should thank heaven that you said those words to me while I was wearing these clothes. Do you understand?"

Frightened, she nodded her head, determined not to speak in confidence anymore. She didn't ask pardon, and this perhaps pleased the fierce man, striking him that he had taught her a lesson about dignity. But then the discussion took on a different tone: he became once again the inquisitor, and pressed her about whether she really knew nothing about Aroldo.

"Nothing."

"And do you know who has spread the story that Signor Aroldo is living like a bandit?"

"I don't know."

"I can tell you: it's the Giordanos. You haven't seen them again?"

"No."

She really would have liked to rebel, to say that the Giordanos would do better to mind their own business and think about poor Serafino who was going to the other world; but she didn't open her mouth or raise her eyes. And that also pleased the man, who began once again to love her and almost pity her. She was alone, she was assailed like a doe in her lair. He would have liked to defend her, because this was also his duty.

"For my part, I don't believe much in that silly talk. Those Giordanos, old and young, are people of fantasy, and they'll also end up looking for trouble. At any rate, it's good to be aware of everything. And if I come here to bother you, Signorina, it's in your interest. This affair needs to be settled immediately, for everybody's sake. And you should make yourself willing to help the process of justice; it's the act of a clear conscience."

Now Concezione was also moved. That was exactly what she had wanted to do, but nothing came out right, and her clear conscience told her not to express useless suspicions. All the same, she said that Aroldo really had been very much in love with her, and that she had refused him for her own personal reasons, and that on that night before his disappearance, she had really, mercifully, covered him with Maria Giuseppa's cloth.

Then she blushed, made an effort, and told him about the subterranean passage. With surprise, she saw the sergeant laugh.

"Old legends, Signorina. They blossom everywhere there is a little country church, a tower, a ruin. Sometimes they really exist, these subterranean passages, but in real castles. Here, believe me, there is nothing. Your revered ancestors had natural caves and labyrinths at their service, and didn't need to scratch the earth. At any rate, I have my doubts about the departure of Aroldi to other shores. At the time of his disappearance he only had a little bit of money, and if he had set out on foot we would know about it by now. I rather think . . . Tell me the whole truth: you really didn't talk with him, even drunk, the night before he disappeared?"

She stared at him, quickly, with wild eyes; she understood, shook her head, did not reply. He went on, "For a moment I also believed in the guilt of the imbecile Alivia; anything is possible. And I was excited about following the clue of a simple thread from the blanket. But, when I interrogated Alivia, I was almost convinced that he was stupidly innocent; and Signora Maria Giuseppa has found not one, but a hundred alibis for him. Even so, you just can't trust those people. We have to find another path. I have already sniffed it out, and, if I wanted to, I could find the young man immediately, within a quarter of an hour. I haven't done it out of consideration for you, yes, you yourself, Concezione."

It was the first time he had called her by her name only, with an almost paternal accent; and she wanted to cry, to kiss his hand. She satisfied herself by smiling at him, and this was for him the best reward.

"Listen, Concezione, this is not about a crime, nor about any of the fantasies spread around by curious and excited people. Finding the unfortunate youth, shall we say, by public means, would be such a scandal for this little town that it would bring everything down to the ridiculous detriment of those of us who have looked for him for so long, and would harm you, Signorina. Aroldi needs to go away in secret, and write from the first place he comes to, and that way everything can end peacefully. But there is only one person who can persuade him to do this, and you know who it is."

"But why? But how has he managed to hide himself for so long? Who's been feeding him? Tell me. Tell me."

He looked at her intently; and all of a sudden, she bit the knuckle of her index finger.

She had understood. And a rush of jealousy bit her heart like her teeth had bitten her finger. Then she turned livid with anger, and almost with shame. Shame for that wretch, unworthy of her, shame for having suffered for him, for having fantasized about him, for having so uselessly lowered and humiliated herself. And now she had to save him? Oh no, let him sink in his own darkness and mud, let him go to hell live and well.

"Go on, cause a scandal," she said to the sergeant. "I'm not moving."

He looked at her with his round, shining eyes like black diamonds. He said, slowly, "That night, Aroldi, when he sobered up, went down to town and went in a house. He took a knife and cut the veins of his wrists. He was hidden in a hayloft and saved with difficulty; he had lost almost all his blood. He's still there, but he keeps trying to redo the evil deed. It really is necessary to save him and make him leave. Now have you understood, Concezione?"

She had understood, but she asked for time to decide.

"Come back tomorrow evening," she said. "Let me think. Now I am too stunned."

Whether of his own accord, or because of the suggestion of others, the phlebotomy doctor returned the next day. He wore his overcoat, which stank of benzene, tightly buttoned up, his gloves with holes in the fingers, his dandy cane, and a sly look on his face like a wrinkled, worm-eaten pear. His eyes were also unusually bright, as if they too had been newly cleaned with benzene. Concezione understood immediately that he too knew Aroldo's secret, but she didn't want to prod him, so she waited for him to speak on his own. And, when she offered him coffee and cookies, she noticed that this time he didn't have an urgent need for nourishment; this must mean that he had already eaten somewhere else, or had gotten some money.

"How young you look," she said, to flatter him and make him talk. "What have you done? Are you in love?"

"If I am, I have been for a long time by now. I have always been in love, ever since I was a year old."

"With your wet nurse?'

"That's right. With my wet nurse. My mother used to say that when I was barely one week old, I would hear her footsteps when she came, since she didn't live in our house, and I would open my mouth like a little bird. And when I grew up, truly, I fell in love for real: she was a beautiful woman, by Bacchus, dark, tall, with braids like those of the ancient damsels who let them hang out of the window so that their lovers could climb up on them."

Concezione laughed so hard that she had to bend over to stop; and in doing so, she remembered her illness and stiffened. What did all of this matter to her, after all—the old man, from whom she hoped for more precise news than what she already knew, and Aroldo himself, now that she knew he was alive and safe?

But the doctor himself wanted to chat.

"I have been to visit poor Serafino. Not that I went there of my own free will, since I am not in the habit of seeking out the sick; but because he had me called to him. He really is in a pitiful state; he has only a few days left to live. But his spirit is alive, very much alive, like a flame that's about to die that suddenly blazes up higher, ready for the flight into the void. You could say that he's happy. And he is, in fact, because as the poet says, the only really beautiful thing after love is death. To leave our disgusting bodies and fly among great, pure, eternal things. That's it. I don't believe in what they call God, but, after all, to die is to go back into the joy of the universe. Serafino, though, is worried about the fate of Costante Alivia. He says that he is innocent, and that they're keeping him in jail most of all because that imbecile likes it and because of the reputation of the police, who will put him back on the street as soon as they have news of Aroldi. To this end, Serafino says you could help everyone and bring a happy ending to this tragicomedy."

"I?"

"Yes, you, dear. No one knows better than you do that the idiot is innocent."

"Maybe he is, but how to prove it? You could do it better than I could, doctor. Perhaps you know where Signor Aroldi is hiding."

The doctor tossed his cane into the air and caught it again, without replying. With a serious voice, she continued, "But nobody wants all these stories to be over more than I do. I want my life to be peaceful again, and I also want poor Serafino to go peacefully. For him, therefore, and also to assuage my conscience, I am willing to do whatever he advises."

The doctor bowed his head and rested his chin on the knob of the cane.

"Listen," he said, "I'm going to take a little walk now. In the meantime, your mother will come back; then I will come get you and we will go to Serafino together."

"I can't go until this evening. I'm expecting someone first."

Everyone was in agreement, therefore, that this "story" should end in the best way possible. And when the sergeant dropped by again, she told him that she was ready for anything, without hiding the fact that poor Serafino also wanted to see her and give her some advice.

He seemed opposed, indeed, even a bit jealous; but since it had to do with a dying man, he gave her permission to go visit him.

"But you must promise me, Signorina, not to do anything without consulting me first. I'll find a way for you to have a talk with Signor Aroldi, and I will look after the expenses of his departure. I'll be back here tomorrow morning."

She promised, and when the doctor came back, she wrapped herself up well in her shawl and tied her shoes well, as if she were going on a long journey.

It was a warm, clear night. The full moon rose over the mountains, big and bright as if new. In the moonlight the woods glittered with silver reflections, like a petrified waterfall. The road in front of the doctor and Concezione also seemed like the dried up bed of a stream, with the outline of the town at the bottom, detached against a turquoise sky, with many threads of smoke, equal in size, shining like the pipes of an organ. It was truly a night like the night of the manger,* or of enchantment, with the humid smell of acanthus and sorrel, and an occasional flame that rose up and went out in the bluish distance of the valley like a will-'o-the-wisp.

"Aren't you going to give me your arm, then?" said the doctor, who actually clung to Concezione out of fear of stumbling. "I'll tell you a story. On a moonlit night like this one, I passed this way with a woman. It wasn't a lover's stroll, no; imagine, between her and me we were about a hundred years old, and I was thirty, so figure it out. But we were going to a meeting: the woman's son was a fugitive, a killer, and he was dying a miserable death of carbuncles, in a hiding place above your little church, not far from the rock where Signor Aroldo disappeared. I had taken care of the sick man, but I had been called too late. Now he was dying, and he didn't want a priest; he only wanted to see his mother again. We arrived at the place; the mother sat down beside her son, on the ground, and took his hand. They didn't say a word. They stayed like that for almost an hour, until I said it was time to go. The old woman stood up, and I saw an incredible thing: the sick man regained a natural color, sat up, and asked for something to drink. I accompanied the old woman back to her house, and she didn't even thank me. The next day, the sick man, miraculously cured, went back up there with the wild boars and the rocks; the old woman was found dead, with a mysterious infection of the blood. Do you understand? With her will, with the strength of her love, she had absorbed the poison from the body of her son, and she had saved him."

Concezione shivered; it seemed like one of the usual stories of the phlebotomist, but still she shivered. If it weren't for stories like this, maybe the world would be even worse than it is.

Serafino lay in a little bed that looked like a cradle, a poor little wax angel whose wings had been torn off and who was

---

* *Una vera notte da presepio:* a night like the night Jesus was born.

gradually melting into a cold sweat. All around him there weighed a funerary silence. The Giordano house had at any rate something mysterious about it, like the refuge of people who wanted to hide at all costs. A wall almost higher than the building itself enclosed the stony courtyard. It was totally covered with aloe plants and crowned with a barbaric diadem of pieces of glass that in the light of the moon gave off ironic green, red, and yellow sparks like precious stones. Meanwhile, the little house, small and dark, with small doors, little windows, and shutters each different from the others, seemed like a dwelling place of dwarfs and elves, an impression intensified by a crooked fig tree from which fell great black leaves accompanied by the strange chirping of fantastic birds. Serafino's mother resembled Concezione's mother, but with a tragic air that was justified, after all, by her son's painful state. She received the two visitors in perfect silence, bringing them in not, as she usually did, through the hospitable kitchen, but through a cold, dark passageway, and then up a small stone staircase, all one flight. The door of Serafino's room was open, and out of it came a mixed smell of church and pharmacy. A small oil lamp on the wooden shelf of the chest illuminated a little painting of a Madonna who was also nocturnal and almost veiled with fog; but overhead, on the white wall, a crucifix of gilded metal shone like a sword.

Concezione drew near the little white bed almost with a bound, and saw Serafino's big eyes grow wider, like those of a boy waking up from a dream. His face of yellowish alabaster seemed illuminated by the moon. It was an internal light which turned a light blue color when the sick man recognized Concezione; but his mouth was bitter and his swollen lips seemed to have retained the taste and the black color of his vomited blood. Without a sound, moving his head back and forth on the pillow as if to free himself from an unwanted wrapping, he gave Concezione a sign to be seated. She sat down and she realized that they had been left alone.

"I have come," she said right away, so as not to weary him, "to find out what I should do."

And she bent towards him, as if making her confession. But to her amazement, Serafino's voice rang out loud. It was, though, a voice she didn't recognize, as if it came from far away, from the depths of a ravine.

"Listen: there is a man, a Christian, who has run the greatest risk that one of God's creatures can run, the risk of losing his soul. You must save him. The danger is still great."

"I know—he tried to kill himself."

"Yes, but that's not all there is to it: the woman who hid him, more not to be bothered by the law than out of pity; who covered him with straw like they cover snow so it doesn't melt; who called and paid the phlebotomist to take care of him and save him, now asks an adequate repayment of him. She wants them to leave together, to migrate like the birds, but without getting married. She wants her freedom even while she holds that of the wretched man in her fist; and this, Concezione, is the greater danger. He must leave by himself, flee alone. The first step has been taken: he is now here, in my house. You have to see him."

She hung her head, humbled. She was afraid to see Aroldo; and now that she knew he was alive, safe, she seemed to feel no more passion for him.

"But why don't you let them go away together? They'll end up getting married, like so many others, who start out as friends . . . "

"You don't know, my daughter. You may have made some mistakes, but you don't know about life. Aroldo was able to escape unnoticed from her lair this evening because the woman was entertaining another man. That sort of woman cannot get married, not to a man who ought to save his own soul. And besides, if he were in love with her—love purifies everything. But he thinks only about another woman, and only for this other woman he has done many crazy things."

"But I can't marry him either."

"I'm not telling you to marry him. I'm telling you to make him go away. Only you can give him back his courage, save him from desperation."

She wrung her hands, more desperate than Aroldo. Finally she made up her mind, since it was necessary to put an end to it, and drink the bitter cup to the dregs.

"I'll tell him everything. I'll tell him that a terrible illness separates me from him and from the rest of the world."

"Illness and health are in God's hands," responded Serafino, but now his voice was low, like a flame going out. "I also have a terrible illness, yet I am happy because it's a trial God has chosen to send me on this earth. Now I am about to enter into his kingdom, and I am content. That's what will happen to you if you do your duty, if you sow good around you. Now it's about saving a soul. Go."

She got up. Her shadow covered the bed, falling over Serafino's body; and he raised his arms, let them fall on her shadow and seemed to caress it.

"I really am happy," he murmured, and he closed his eyes. Now that he had finished his last good deed, he had the impression that he could fall asleep like a weary wayfarer, on the grass, in the shade of a tree.

Concezione went out on tiptoe and groped her way down the staircase. She felt like she was dreaming, walking among ghosts. And, truly, the man sitting in front of the fire in the smoky kitchen looked like a ghost. She recognized him by his gray suit, the same that he had worn the day he came to visit her, but worn-out, large, floppy, like it too had been sick. A scarf of the same color was wrapped around Aroldo's neck, a neck grown as thin as that of a plucked bird. And his thin face, with its still, tired eyes, was the same color. But when she put a hand on his shoulder, he seemed to awaken from a sad dream; his hands shook, his eyes took on light again, even if it was the light of tears.

And Serafino's mother and the phlebotomist, who, sitting at the table drank from time to time from a pitcher full of wine, disappeared suddenly, silently. Concezione sat down next to the stranger. Yes, he seemed a stranger again, like the first time she saw him, no longer the Aroldo she had dreamed about that summer in a delirium of love. The passion of her body had fallen like the leaves; and to see him so pale and aged, long and fragile like a reed, she felt an almost physical repugnance. But her heart beat all the same, with a feeling akin to the tenderness awakened by a distant, vague, unreachable music that makes you cry with sadness as well as with joy, and that you would like to recognize, to understand the meaning of, but you can't, like you can't catch birds in flight. She thought again about the poor women who came to her little house to ask alms and warm themselves by the fire of her hearth and of her charity; Aroldo too had become a needy person, needier than those women, and she felt the joy of being able to do him a bit of good. After having stripped him and martyred him, it's true, but not by her own fault.

"Aroldo," she said immediately, "I have to ask your forgiveness for what has happened to you. Believe me, it's not my fault; and when I've told you the truth, you'll see that the major fault was in fact not telling you about it right away. I told you that I was sick, but I didn't say with what illness. It's a sickness that, like leprosy, like tuberculosis, is still incurable. And they say it's passed on to one's children. The worst obstacle of all, therefore, for a person of conscience, is that it separates you from those who love you. When I met you I didn't know I had it; that's why, afterwards, I behaved towards you like a capricious and fickle woman. There is a kind of shame in talking about certain illnesses, in showing the intimate wounds of the body. I have had this shame, forgetting that Jesus made of his wounds the lamps that illumine the world more than the sun and the stars. There—that's all."

Aroldo bent over; with his elbows on his knees and his face in his hands, he looked like a child who wanted to hide, but Concezione realized that he was crying. She let him vent, since she knew that tears are the best medicine for a serious pain. She knew it, even if she never managed to cry. And the pain of that man was deep, inexpressible with words. It resembled that music that Concezione heard rise up out of her heart, as if from the depths of the valleys, in the days of her first love, when she had heard the very voice of life echoing in the murmuring of the water, the grass, the wind. But the man's weeping was a still deeper and stronger music than the music and the songs of love. It was the voice of the sea during a storm, that swallows up the poor innocent fishermen, the voice of the lightning that splits the pure trees, the voice of children violated and killed by human monsters, the voice of the sicknesses that God sends to humans to make them taste, in the end, like a priceless prize, the sleep of death. It was the voice of sorrow.

Then the young man tried to rebel: he raised himself, also ashamed of his weeping, and said in a harsh voice, "You'll get well, Concezione. They'll find some cure. If you have faith, you'll get well. Remember that sermon of Serafino in the little church . . . "

"Yes, the boy was cured because Jesus wanted him to be. But then he also died, that boy; he's been dead for almost two thousand years, yet he still lives and plays alongside us. And we will also get well, Aroldo, with God's will, after our deaths. And now, listen, we need, in fact, to talk about eternal life. You are sicker than I am, Aroldo; your soul is sick; and you need to save it. You have to go away from this town, but by yourself, without seeing that woman again. There are those who will help you get away. And you can be in peace about me, because I will always think about you. Like a brother," she added, to not start again on the road of illusions.

"Why should I run away? I'll never go back to that woman, you can be sure of that, nor will she come to carry me away on her shoulders. Anyway, you've probably understood it correctly: I went to her so as to insult and spite you; it was the greatest disrespect I could show you. If I had gone out of love I wouldn't have done what I did. And she took advantage of it; because in her heart she has the hatred of Cain for you; and even she's not to blame."

"No one is to blame for their own evils, but it's better to avoid temptations."

He struck his knee with his fist, and went on, raising his voice.

"No, I won't go. Because I have committed an act of weakness, must I always be weak? You learn more from your errors than from your virtues."

"The sergeant . . . "

"I couldn't care less about the sergeant. He's the one who looks foolish, and I can't do anything about that. What does he have to reproach me about? I have been sick; now I am better. Tomorrow I will report back to the manager, and if he wants me, I'll go back to work. And if he doesn't, I'll look elsewhere. I'll go back to knife sharpening, if I have to, and I'll think about my mother as though she were still alive and I still needed to help her. And, yes, this will keep me from temptation."

"Serafino also wants you to go."

"No!" he shouted, and then bent over again as though afraid of his own voice. "Why should I go? That woman never leaves her house; but if she were to come to look for me on the street I would know how to put her in her place. I know how much she has done for me, and if some day she should need anything I would also help her, but like a good Christian and nothing else. But I swear to you, Concezione, I swear to you on the memory of my mother, I will never go back to her house for any indecent reason. Nor will I ever go back to your house, I promise you; unless you call me back. Because . . . "

"Because?" she asked, once more restless and sad.

"Listen, Concezione. I have to tell you everything. The doctor took care of me, then, secretly. He's good at these secret cures because, he'll tell you so himself, he's used to them. He said, 'But look at what I need to do: I who drew blood have to try to put it back into your foolish veins. You need a transfusion of blood, and I can do it, too, better than those asses at the hospital. But where will we find the Christian who will give you his blood? We could try with that of a sheep, but you are already enough of a sheep.' Then that woman offered hers. I have to admit it, she is generous when necessary, generous like a brigand. Those are the doctor's words too. But

I didn't accept it; rather, I wanted to start over, to end it. And if I didn't try to kill myself again, believe me, it was out of gratitude for my hostess, since I didn't want to create any problems for her with the police, and also because she couldn't bury me secretly. But I wasn't able to move, because I was too weak to stand on my feet, and she watched over my prison. I thought, 'There's still time, and as soon as I can I will go to some solitary place where they will find my carcass stripped by the vultures.' But the doctor came and forced me to drink some of his concoctions that gave me my blood back. I think he made me drink the blood of a just slaughtered ox, and he made me eat so much raw liver and so many eggs that I will never again in my life taste liver or eggs. But he knew the best cure; and when the woman left us alone, he talked to me about you. We would be in the dark, because he came at night and only a little light came in from the skylight of the hayloft. I didn't understand why the woman, who owned neither horses nor oxen, had a hayloft, but the doctor explained it to me. She had built it some time ago precisely to hide a fugitive friend. And she did it so well that also that time the man was able to stay there safely all winter. Then she got bored, and he also preferred to take off and hide in the free air of the mountains. The doctor, then, brought me news of you. He told me that you thought about me all the time, that you loved me, that you were consumed for me."

"What did he know, the old meddler?" she protested, but she blushed, because it was the truth.

"He knew, he knew. Some things can't be hidden, and where there's smoke, there's fire. I thought I was dreaming, and, anyway, thrown into continual drowsiness by the weakness, I always dreamed about you. But it was more like a hallucination. You came, you sat on the hay next to me, and you did not speak. But you looked at me, and your eyes were so bright that the hayloft seemed brightened by the sun. I, who was always cold, grew warm. And so, little by little, through this magic more than anything else, I didn't think about dying any more. Now . . . "

"Now . . . ?"

"Things are upside down. Now you're the one who says you are sick, or at least that you are afraid of becoming gravely ill. Let's hope that doesn't happen. God can work miracles, and I will pray for you day and night. And if you want to be left in peace by me, you will be. But if, God forbid, you should become really sick, and you want to call me, I'll be at your feet like a dog; and I'll look at you like you looked at me in the dream. I am sure that the light of my eyes will make you well."

She smiled, with a pale, sad smile.

"These are the doctor's whims, Aroldo; he tells his silly tales well. But life is not a silly tale."

"And yet," said Aroldo, imitating her smile, "if Grandfather Giordano thought we two were sitting here in front of his fireplace, he also would think he was dreaming."

"And he would run down with his stick to send us away in a fury of blows. Better, then, to go soon of our own free will. Me first, then you. But first, I insist that we agree on something: you must go far away. Serafino is even prepared to pay for your trip, until you have found work."

He turned his face towards her, and it was a livid, hard face that she had never seen.

"Now you offend me, Concezione. You all offend me. And, by God, it's right: I have done something only cowardly men can do. But maybe I have also done some good: my blood has been changed. The doctor says that among you people here, the children and sometimes some of the adults eat the liver of a just slaughtered beast, still hot and smoking, in order to become courageous. And he has nourished me with raw liver and the blood of an animal; so I too have become a bit strong. Maybe I am also a bit of a beast, but strong and courageous, even if wild. I don't accept alms from anybody. Tomorrow I will begin to work again: I'll break rocks, I'll suffer hunger, I'll sleep on the ground. But being poor doesn't mean being miserable. I'll never be a beggar. Never. Never."

His words fell slow, soft, but firm and inexorable, and Concezione, deep down, was happy and proud. She felt that yesterday's boy had become a man, like the young soldier who has been in war. And now he had really taken on something of her people: tenacious in hatred and in evil, but also in love and for the good.

"And now, let's say good-bye, and may God be with us."

She got up; she didn't even stretch out her hand to him. And he did not move.

The moon had risen in the clear sky; but for the already bare branches of the trees and the sound of the creek on the side of the mountain it would have seemed like a summer's night.

In front of the open gate, Concezione noted that someone must have come during her absence, but she was not alarmed.

"It must be that crazy Comare Maria Giuseppa. She travels even at night, like the witches."

"Or like the fairies," said the phlebotomist. "Who knows how much good stuff she has brought. Tell me, Concezione, won't you invite me to dinner, by any chance?"

"Just imagine! But won't you be afraid to go back by yourself?"

"Am I less than a woman? And look at the weapons I have: I have a scalpel to draw blood, and if that shoemaker the other day was able to kill a thief with an awl, I can also defend myself against my enemies. But now let's drop these sad stories: what a good smell is coming out of your kitchen!"

Bent over the fire, the old woman in fact was roasting a fat, fragrant sausage on a spit. Other fresh sausages lay on the table, and surrounded by those pink and brown harmless serpents, there arose a little plaster Madonna, the kind sold by traveling salesmen. Yes, it was clear that Comare Maria Giuseppa Alivia had been there.

"She didn't even get off her horse, she only held out to me a package of sausages and this statue, which she carried on her saddlebow, like a baby. She said she had been notified that

Costante would be freed from jail tomorrow morning, and she had come to get him. She went off, spurring her horse like at the horse races."

"Provided that tomorrow her charming nephew really doesn't try to kill his rival. But one could say this to him: 'You are killing a dead man.' "

"Not really," Concezione almost protested, but she let it go.

The phlebotomist was unusually cheerful; he even seemed to have grown younger. He thought he was the central character of the story that had just ended, at least for the moment, to everyone's relief. He had no illusions about the fact that the following day life would start again all the same, with small and big tribulations for those who were still alive and at grips with their fellow creatures. Life is an adventure that ends only with death. But in the meantime, after years of injustices, of abandonment, and of misery, he had once more enjoyed a bit of his old prestige, gotten himself mixed up in an unusual event, and in some way cooperated for the good of his faithful clients.

He closed the door, approached the table, sniffed the sausages, and picked up the little statue that, although it was almost half a meter tall, was hollow and light as a doll. Then he sat down by the fire, attempting to calm Giustina's curiosity by telling her only a part of Aroldo's adventures.

"That night, what with sleeping outside and the heat of his drunkenness on him, he caught a long, stubborn pleurisy. Still tipsy, he took refuge with Maria Pasqua. She couldn't believe it—she could hide him and keep him prisoner with the hope of making whatever she wanted of him. We should have pity on her; she's also a sad and unbalanced creature, alone in this disgusting wide world, persecuted in her lair like a filthy fox. And I won't deny that she has the instincts of a fox. She's also descended from certain folks, with the difference that it's not really her fault that she is."

This time, though, so that her mother would not be mortified any further, Concezione thought it wise to intervene. "Let's let it be. Everything is over now."

In the meantime, she set the table. Then she took the little statue into the church. Only the light from the little lamp illuminated the cold, sad place; but Concezione, kneeling on the bare pavement, remembered Aroldo's words: "Your eyes, in the darkness, were so bright that the hayloft seemed brightened by the sun."

And now that's how they looked. They had an unquenchable light that came from her soul, that, even when her eyes were closed forever, would never go out.

Translator's
Afterword

Grazia Deledda (1871–1936)

In 1900, when Grazia Deledda, twenty-nine years old and newly married, left Sardinia for Rome, she already had sixteen books in print. By the time of her death thirty-six years later, she was the author of over sixty volumes, including novels, collections of stories and folklore of Sardinia, poetry, and essays. Two things about this life of literature are truly remarkable: the fact that, although Deledda spent more than half her life in Rome, the location of most of her fiction is Sardinia; and the degree of anonymity in which Deledda lived and worked, in spite of the level of international recognition that came with the Nobel Prize in Literature awarded to her in 1926. Deledda was only the second Italian author (after Giosuè Carducci in 1906), and is still the only Italian woman writer, to have been so honored. And yet, by her own choice, she lived and worked in obscurity; even her death was barely noted in the Italian press. Deledda died on August 15, 1936. The first notice of her death in Milan's prestigious daily newspaper *Corriere della sera* was a brief note on August 18, reporting on the funeral held in Rome the day before and explaining that the writer had asked her family to announce her death only to a closed circle of friends.[1]

It is clear that the two obsessions of Deledda's life, Sardinia and privacy, are closely related to her strong, eccentric personality. Grazia Deledda grew up in Nuoro, a rather remote provincial capital in the center of the island. She was a middle-class child and an autodidact. She gorged on fiction, especially nineteenth-century French and Russian novels, throughout her childhood, and published her first novel, *Sangue Sardo (Sardinian Blood)* at fifteen, and her first collection of stories (her earliest work still in print) when she was nineteen years old.[2] Deledda left an account of her bookish girlhood in the posthumously published autobiographical novella, *Cosima,* a tender reminiscence of a young girl caught between the romance of bandits and heroes of old Sardinia and a gradually awakening intellectual curiosity stifled by the very home she so loved.[3] In 1899, she moved to Cagliari, the largest city in Sardinia; the next year she met and married Palmiro Madesani, a career bureaucrat with whom she moved to Rome. The couple had two sons, Franz and Sardus. It is clear that Madesani provided her an escape to the larger world for which she had longed, but Deledda's later life proved just as clearly that "you can take the girl out of Sardinia, but you can't take Sardinia out of the girl."

The Madesani-Deledda household in Rome was exceptionally private, even reclusive, and a thriving center of literary production. In her first two decades in the capital, Deledda published approximately one novel a year, including some of her more famous works, such as *Dopo il divorzio, Elias Portolu, Cenere, L'edera,* and *Canne al vento.*[4] During this period, Palmiro Madesani gradually became his wife's literary agent. This very unusual combination, a woman author whose husband supported and was supported by her career, inspired a satirical novel by Luigi Pirandello, *Suo marito (Her Husband),* in which a thinly disguised Grazia Deledda appears in the portrait of Silvia Roncella, a woman writer recently arrived in Rome with her husband from Taranto.[5] Deledda seems to have been offended by this book, so out of respect for a fellow writer, Pirandello withdrew it from circulation and did not allow it to be reprinted. When Pirandello died in 1936, some four months after the death of Deledda, he left a partly revised manuscript which was published by his son, Stefano, with the title *Giustino Roncella nato Boggiòlo.*[6] Although the extensive changes to the first four chapters were meant to soften the parody of Deledda, the new title still satirizes the role reversal of the Madesani-Deledda marriage by suggesting that the husband took his wife's name. It is the first version of this book that remains in print, with its vivid ironical portrait of "numberless young Italian women authors: poets, short story writers, novelists (a few of them also playwrights)."[7]

Pirandello may have found the idea of a woman author comical, but the fact of Deledda's Nobel Prize in 1926, eight years before he, for all his greater fame, won the same honor in 1934, was evidence that he had been wise to take her seriously. In fact, Deledda and Pirandello, along with such famous contemporaries as Gabriele d'Annunzio, Pietro Mascagni, and Giovanni Verga, formed part of an artistic and literary circle in Rome associated with the periodical *Nuova Antologia,* although Deledda was a very marginal and reticent member of this group. A reminiscence by an admittedly very minor member of the group, Lucio d'Ambra, was published on *la terza pagina* (the literary page) of the *Corriere della sera* shortly after Deledda's death. It describes her in this literary environment as "tucked into a corner, her hands hidden in a mangy muff, her eyes cast down to the pavement, head down, hoping that the large brim of her feathered hat would be enough to hide her and save her the great difficulty of greeting others. . . . She did not know how to converse. Hers was a silence that listened, like her rough Sardinian mountains that, mutely, hear the sea on all sides."[8]

A decade earlier, when she won the Nobel Prize, an article in the *Corriere della sera* had dubbed her *la Taciturna.*[9]

Grazia Deledda was, then, for all her international fame, little-acknowledged and appreciated in Italy in her own lifetime. This was certainly because of the deeply patriarchal, antifemale bias of Italian letters in the early decades of this century; but it must also be acknowledged to be, at least in part, a result of her own character and personality. She was an author who sought contact with the world through her writing far more than through her personal relationships.

La chiesa della solitudine

If Grazia Deledda is something of an overlooked writer of her generation, the last novel published during her lifetime, *La chiesa della solitudine (The Church of Solitude)*, is certainly her forgotten work.[10] This may be because Deledda is generally known for her earlier works, portraits of the social changes in early twentieth-century Sardinia: the crumbling aristocratic class and the rise of the moneyed bourgeoisie. Furthermore, *La chiesa della solitudine* was overshadowed by the more lighthearted, posthumously published *Cosima*. But the neglect of this novel is certainly also connected to the fact of its unmentionable subject: cancer. On the first page, the protagonist, Maria Concezione, leaves the small hospital of her town:

> She had undergone a serious operation: her left breast had been completely cut away. Upon discharging her, the head physician had said with Olympian and crystalline cruelty, "You are fortunate you are no longer very young—twenty-eight, I believe—so the disease will take some time to come back. Ten years, maybe even twelve. In any case, take good care of yourself: don't overwork, don't seek out emotion. Peace and quiet, right? And let me see you every now and again."
> (p. 1)

The skillful introduction of the subject of cancer, made crystal clear while the word is not mentioned, is one of the central narrative devices of *La chiesa della solitudine*. In fact, the word "cancer" appears only once in the book, slightly past the midpoint, when an old phlebotomist, a leech doctor largely discredited since the establishment of a hospital and scientific medicine in the town, accuses another doctor of telling a woman she had a cancer and cutting away part of her breast just to make money (p. 87).

But, although cancer is almost never spoken of, it is present on every page of the novel; the silence is as deliberate as it is deafening. Deledda even makes her characters ruminate on this rhetoric of the unsaid and unsayable. For example, Concezione and her mother, Maria Giustina,

> spoke about this illness as little as possible, like a mysterious thing. Even its terrible name, that not even the doctors had pronounced clearly, remained deep in their hearts with a secret agreement to never reveal it, not even to themselves. (p. 4)

Precisely because of the impossibility of naming the disease that has changed her life, Concezione finds herself at the center of an ever widening maze of misunderstandings. The person most strongly affected by the changes in her is Aroldo, a young man come to Sardinia from northern Italy (probably Lombardy, the land of the rice fields) to work on the road that is being built to connect Concezione's town to the plains, the sea, to other roads, in short, to the outside world. Aroldo brings the outside world into Concezione's life the way Palmiro Madesani did in Deledda's, but with very different results. His ambition is to emigrate to South America and be part of the foundation of a new city near Patagonia, and he wants to take Concezione with him. Aroldo and Maria Concezione are in love, but however tenderly she related to him before her operation, on her return from the hospital she is a different person:

> He saw the change clearly—she neither displayed it nor hid it; she seemed another person to him too. It was as if the hospital, instead of the operation the two women had described to him—that is, the simple extraction of a nasal polyp—had by witchcraft taken her blood, her flesh, her youth. Something inexplicable, beyond the breath of sorrow and illness, emanated from her, almost a sense of threat and danger, chilling the comforting, hospitable atmosphere of the house. (p. 7)

Concezione's illness makes it impossible for her to go with Aroldo; her inability to speak about her illness makes it impossible for Aroldo to understand the change that has taken place in her. This leads to a series of disasters that, in the mystery story that makes up the last half of the novel, almost costs Aroldo his life. For Concezione, the tragedy of her empty chest, continual reminder of her mortality, and the reason why she cannot marry or even think of having children, is inevitably linked to an earlier tragedy, the imprisonment and suicide of her first love. Just back from the hospital, on her knees before the statue of the Virgin of Solitude, for which the small chapel attached to her house is named, she prays:

> "I should not have children; I shouldn't have any," she thought, among the words of her prayer, "and it's right, it's right. Everything in your will is right, O Lord. I have sinned against love, I have sown pain and destroyed a man's life; and now you sprinkle the salt of sterility on my life, O Lord. Thy will be done. And you, Virgin Mother, help me now to get through this desolate life of mine. Look down on me from the heights of your mercy." (p. 6)

Throughout the novel, Concezione understands her cancer either as a punishment from God for her sins or the sins of her bandit forefathers who had left her wealthy, or as a trial given to her in this life precisely because she is so virtuous. The "good" Maria Concezione and the "bad" Maria Concezione vie with one another throughout the book; this tension is, in fact, one of the central points of her fascination for Aroldo, the old phlebotomist, and her various other suitors. The "bad" Maria Concezione is further personified by her half-sister Maria Pasqua, a fallen woman who never actually appears in the novel, but whose shadow looms over it. The "bad" Maria Concezione attracts people to her, but the "good" Maria Concezione, rigidly encased in her solitude, turns them away. Serafino, the priest who says mass at the Church of Solitude, says to Concezione,

"You know what I should tell you, Maria Concezione? You are a little bit like life. You understand what I mean: everyone looks at life with the hope of receiving pleasure, money, love; but basically life flees from us and gives us nothing but delusions and, often, pain. My grandfather, my brothers, maybe others, look at you because of your fortune, and they think you are a woman who, besides money, can give them happiness. But instead you are a poor creature, weak and unhappy." (p. 35)

The old phlebotomist says to her,

"You know what you have, Maria Concezione? You have the urgent need of a husband."

She laughed, and drew back the hand that he was palpating with his nervous fingers.

"And where will I find this husband?"

"Rascal, daughter of rascals! Where will you find him? Wherever your siren's eyes happen to fall. If you want, I'll send you one, within the hour at the most, at a full gallop." (pp. 62)

Maria Concezione is not an immediately likable protagonist; she is dark, brooding, moody, silent, solitary, as Deledda calls her twice, a "Bedouin" (pp. 1, 104). She is, in fact, something like Grazia Deledda: taller, younger, more beautiful, perhaps, but with the same silent, reclusive personality, the same repeated desire to be left alone. This resemblance is more than accidental, since in 1936, when *La chiesa della solitudine* was published, Grazia Deledda was dying of breast cancer.

The silence of this novel, then, is the silence inscribed in the life and death of the author. As Carla Locatelli has put it, "[T]he dimension of silence in personal and social experience has a determinative power in the construction of the world in which we live."[11] This makes it all the more interesting that *La*

chiesa della solitudine has received so little critical attention, and
that the critics who have spoken about it have also done so by
allusion and periphrasis, carefully avoiding the unspeakable word,
and so continuing the silence. For example, Anna Dolfi says,
"Stricken by the same illness about which she had spoken in
one of her last novels, *La chiesa della solitudine,* Deledda died
in Rome on August 15, 1936. . . . "[12]

But even such elliptical references recognize the fact that
La chiesa della solitudine is, in some way, a novel about Grazia
Deledda's own final illness. This recognition was given a physical form when, in 1959, Deledda's mortal remains were moved
to the little seventeenth-century church of La Madonna della
Solitudine outside of Nuoro, the church which had inspired the
setting of the novel. The author's painstaking descriptions of
the mechanism by which the most important thing is the thing
that remains unsaid have an uncanny consonance with the deep
silences of her own life, and make the silence of criticism all the
more painful.

Illness as Metaphor

This silence is, though, no surprise since, as Susan Sontag
has pointed out, silence is the major metaphor of cancer in the
literature of modern western culture, just as a preternatural
sensitivity is the metaphor of tuberculosis.[13] Sontag argues that
important illnesses, especially those that affect a large number
of people and seem capricious and incurable, tend to take on
another life through literary metaphors. While the metaphors
of tuberculosis and cancer "crisscross and overlap,"[14] each disease has developed a separate metaphorical personality, which
has in turn affected the experience of those who must deal with
disease on a real and personal basis.

Sontag came to this insight while being treated for cancer
in the 1970s, although she insists that her goal is not to de-
scribe the experience of illness but rather to explore the fantasies constructed around it ("not what it is really like to emigrate

to the kingdom of the ill and live there, but the punitive or sentimental fantasies concocted about that situation").[15] In fact, she argues that real illness is *not* a metaphor, and that the "healthiest" way of being ill is to avoid and resist the particular metaphorical world of each illness.

In the western literary tradition of modernity, Sontag sees tuberculosis as the disease around which has been constructed the most complex metaphorical world. Keats, Shelley, Byron, Goldsmith, Stendahl, Poe, Kafka, Dickens, Wolfe, Gide, O'Neill, Henry James, James Joyce, D. H. Lawrence, Katherine Mansfield, Robert Louis Stevenson, Harriet Beecher Stowe, the Bröntes—these are but some of the authors who either lived or created the myth of the noble, innocent, somehow more refined and sensitive tubercular protagonist, consumed with inward burning. Ironically, Sontag argues, the most famous novel of tuberculosis, Thomas Mann's *The Magic Mountain,* is a late, self-conscious reflection on the myth that shows its power but it does not quite believe in it.[16]

The literary metaphors for cancer are more complicated and somewhat contradictory. On the one hand, cancer is a rampant aggression of cells in battle against the body; on the other hand, cancer is connected to stagnation and frustration, to repressed desires and anger and frustrated ambitions. But in one way at least, the difference is clear: tuberculosis is the disease of emotion and excess and beatification; cancer is the disease of secrets and silence and defeat. Sontag points to Tolstoy's *The Death of Ivan Ilyich* as "a case history of the link between cancer and characterological resignation," and notes the number of famous men who somehow lost or compromised something important in their lives and subsequently died of cancer: Napoleon, Ulysses S. Grant, Robert A. Taft, Hubert Humphrey, even Freud and Wittgenstein.[17]

Sontag's meditation on illness as metaphor is particularly valuable and appropriate for an analysis of the works of Grazia Deledda precisely because Deledda's own literary formation was by means of those books which best demonstrate the metaphors of illness at their most grandiose. In fact, a comparison of the respective roles of tuberculosis and cancer in Deledda's later writing will show to what extent she was influenced by, but also used and transcended, the metaphors of illness.

Deledda does, in fact, have a "tuberculosis novel" which could be compared with her "cancer novel." *Il paese del vento,* published in 1931, five years before *La chiesa della solitudine,*[18] is a first-person narration of the early months of the marriage of Nina, who leaves a small town in the mountains to go live by the seaside with her husband. It is easy to see in the portrait of both the bookish young girl and her older, tolerant, but condescending husband the description of young Grazia Deledda portrayed in *Cosima,* who later left Sardinia with Palmiro Madesani.[19] "Nina/Cosima/Grazia" is especially interesting because her authorial (and autobiographical) gaze is not fixed on her husband, but rather on Gabriele, a lost love from her childhood who just happens to be in the same seaside village, dying of tuberculosis. Although Gabriele's disease is not mentioned by name, it is described vividly: he is gaunt, spectral, feverish, he coughs and spits up blood. As a boy, Gabriele had dreamed of going to Germany to study medicine and find a cure for tuberculosis, now he is instead totally consumed by it.

Gabriele is an autobiographical figure, an echo of Deledda's tormented infatuation with Stanis Manca, Duke of Asinara, a famous Roman journalist. In 1891, out of curiosity, Manca went to Nuoro to meet this strange, reclusive young woman who managed to have her work published on the mainland; he subsequently wrote an article about Deledda, characterizing her as "our little Georges Sand." She maintained a romantic obsession for him even after her marriage to Madesani, nine years later; he, for his part, kept her love letters, which were eventually published.[20] The name "Gabriele" is a literary testimony to the most eminent (and romantic) figure of the Italian literary scene of the 1930s, Gabriele d'Annunzio.

The character of Gabriele in *Il paese del vento* shows Deledda's familiarity with the literary metaphor of tuberculosis, but gives it a darker twist. In the new bride's fantasy and memory, Gabriele is everything the tubercular protagonist should be:

delicate, handsome, sensitive, musical, intelligent, the aesthetic young man she had met briefly and loved deeply as a girl. But when Nina meets Gabriele on the windy beach, he has changed into something dark and somehow evil, something she also understands by way of literary models: "I had read that invalids of his type are evil, and, in the last stage of their disease, can become criminals."[21] The real Gabriele, dying alone in a windy town, has become the opposite of the romantic boy Nina remembered: he is a dark, malignant seabird, with yellow teeth, feverish eyes, bad breath, and evil intentions towards her. In the climactic scene of the novel, when Nina visits Gabriele alone in his rented room, he bitterly accuses her of being the cause of his illness, grabs her by the shoulders, and tries to kiss her.[22] The romantic metaphor of tuberculosis is thus exploded, shown to be as unreal as the fancies of a young girl, and Nina finds comfort in the stolid but healthy figure of her husband.

There is also a tubercular character in *La chiesa della solitudine*, the young priest, Serafino. Serafino is hardly a dashing figure: throughout the novel, he is repeatedly described as weak, sickly, pale, waxy. His illness is never named, but, like Gabriele's, it is described clearly:

> The little priest had to take to his bed because the first cold weather, and the religious labors from which he never excused himself—getting up at dawn for mass, teaching catechism to children and women— had reopened the holes in his lungs. He had vomited blood, and now he lay exhausted on his little bed of a virgin martyr, tormented more by the inability to continue his works of charity than by his illness. (p. 132)

In some ways, Serafino does fit a literary metaphor of tuberculosis: he is the spiritual sick person, in contrast to Concezione's striking physicality. Deledda makes use of Serafino's malady to play on the two different literary metaphors of illness, tuberculosis and cancer. This tends to intensify Concezione's isolation.

Even though Serafino is her best friend, Concezione remains unable to speak to him freely about her cancer; his illness is too much of a contrast to hers. Part of this hesitation, of course, is linked to the perception of sexuality related to a disease of the breast. Concezione is ashamed of her illness.

Along with metaphors of illness, *La chiesa della solitudine* makes some interesting observations about metaphors of healing. As the book opens, Concezione is leaving the hospital; in spite of the doctor's command that she return occasionally for check ups, she never goes back. Her experiences in the hospital, the attitude of the doctors, especially the primary physician who speaks to her so coldly and insensitively when she is discharged, the scientific medical profession altogether, become symbols of pain and sorrow she wishes only to leave behind. On her first night back from the hospital, she has a dream in which she escapes from the hospital and, on a moonlit road in a landscape of dreams, loses the blanket in which she has wrapped herself, and finds herself face-to-face with the two men she has loved, the tragic young suicide, and Aroldo. (pp. 26–27)

The hospital, the doctors, the world of scientific cures, can only promise more suffering and, eventually, death. But Maria Concezione yearns for life; she understands her illness, in fact, as a result of not living her life fully. At Easter, while bathing and making herself new for the holiday, Concezione feels the pull of life:

> In spite of the mutilated breast and the memory of the warnings of the doctor at the hospital, Serafino's words and counsels gave her a flush of joy. To live—she wanted to live, to love, to forget her sorrows and her scruples. (p. 66)

Later on, meditating on the tragic story of her first love, she laments her inability to give herself fully, a fault which led to his downfall as much as her own:

> "To flee with him, sin with him, love, suffer, have children and work for them!" The nurse in that damned

hospital had told her that if she had nursed a child the disease would not have come; and the boy with eyes like stars would not have minted counterfeit money and would not have hanged himself like Judas. (p. 97–98)

And, at the end of the novel, when Concezione confronts Aroldo with the fact of her (still unnamed) illness, she again expresses her grief over the way in which it makes her unable to live a normal woman's life:

"It's a sickness that, like leprosy, like tuberculosis, is still incurable. And they say it's passed on to one's children. The worst obstacle of all, therefore, for a person of conscience, is that it separates you from those who love you." (p. 144)

In this way, Deledda invests her protagonist with an understanding of the ancient myth that connects breast cancer with childlessness and melancholy, a myth, as Sontag notes, that goes back to Galen.[23] It is this metaphor of illness that brings into sharper profile the alternative medical figure of the novel, the old phlebotomist. Like the doctors in the hospital, this character is unnamed; but unlike the doctors, he has a strong personality, and is full of theories and opinions about life. He is like a boy in his appreciation for the miracles of nature (a quality he shares with Scrafino).[24] Although the old doctor's bloodletting cures have been thoroughly discredited by the medical profession, so much so that he first appears in the novel starving, neglected, and semi-alcoholic, his philosophy of healing through an exchange of power (love, sex, blood)[25] gradually gains credence, and he does eventually save Aroldo's life. The old phlebotomy doctor exudes a sensuality that Concezione finds repugnant; he represents the power of sexuality as the ultimate pharmacon, both the poison and the cure.

At the end of the novel, Concezione and the phlebotomist walk together into her mother's warm, fragrant kitchen, and so the novel ends with the mirror image of the first page, on which Concezione sets out alone, away from the hospital and the cold, disdainful doctor. Like many modern cancer patients, Concezione wrestles with the competing claims of western science and older, more organic (in twentieth-century terms, "alternative," "Eastern," or "natural") systems of cures. The character of the old phlebotomist is evidence of Deledda's understanding of the enduring power of the metaphors of illness.

Body and Soul: The Power of Love

In *La chiesa della solitudine,* healing is not just a physical process, but also involves a person's soul. Although Deledda is not primarily thought of as a religious writer, many of her books include portraits of the religious lives of her characters; and it is worth noting that her now little-known religious novel *La fuga in Egitto (The Flight into Egypt)* was specifically cited when she won the Nobel Prize.[26] As is only to be expected in a novel set in a church (in fact, every scene takes place either in or just outside of the house/church shared by Concezione and Giustina), religion plays a significant role in *La chiesa della solitudine.* The dominating religious presence is, of course, la Madonna della Solitudine, the statue of the Virgin Mary for whom the church is named. This little Madonna is not particularly attractive (in fact, Concezione feels an emotional attraction only to the *feet* of the infant Jesus) but the most private and intense prayers of both Concezione and Aroldo are directed to her. Their prayers, though, are exactly contradictory and opposed: Aroldo prays for a relief to his loneliness, while Concezione repeatedly asks to be left alone. In this way, the Madonna della Solitudine becomes a neutral religious symbol who is made into whatever the believer wants her to be. Gradually, over the course of the novel, Maria Concezione, remote, stern, alone, becomes the Madonna of Solitude.

A stronger symbolic presence is exerted by the statue of the suffering Christ that Concezione lovingly deposes in a Holy Sepulchre during Easter week. Since the Madonna della Solitudine is ensconced at the altar, this crucifix usually hangs, "tired and resigned" on the wall of the church. But stretched out on the beautifully woven blanket kept just for that purpose, surrounded by sprouted wheat and spring wildflowers, the suffering Christ becomes a powerful symbol of resurrection, profoundly moving to all who see it. As Concezione is filled with tenderness and compassion for Christ, she immediately thinks of the sufferings of Aroldo. When her mother's friend, Comare Maria Giuseppa, brings her a beautifully woven blanket which she hopes will cover the nuptial bed of Concezione and her nephew Costante, Concezione instead imagines it under the dead Christ. Once again, even more forcefully, she makes a connection between Aroldo and the dead Jesus. But then, when Aroldo turns up on the boulders outside of their yard, drunk, truculent, and incoherent, and Maria Concezione covers him with that famous blanket, she takes care to turn it inside out.

The story of Aroldo really does come near to death and resurrection, especially at the end of the novel when the old phlebotomist saves his life by making him drink blood. But the contrast to this dark, spiritualized image is Aroldo the troubadour, the romantic "Childe Harold" of Concezione's fantasies. He chooses this image for himself, both by emphasizing his peripatetic life and, very plainly, by purchasing a guitar. When Giustina sees him stretched out in his drunken stupor, guitar at his side, the authorial voice comments,

> And, if she had known about literature, good Giustina might have compared the youth to a wandering troubadour who, after crossing the dark forests of the mountains, rests before starting out again on his capricious journey. (p. 95)

The phlebotomy doctor actually does make the connection: "Aroldo—a nice name, like a troubadour, and he even has a mandolin" (p. 121). Aroldo Aroldi, "nobody's son," is both the perpetually wandering stranger—nobody—and the emblematic sufferer who comes back from the dead—Everyman.

If the portraits of Maria Concezione and Aroldo go back and forth between the spirit and the flesh, there is one character, Comare Maria Giuseppa Alivia, whose presence in the novel is entirely representative of the world of physical possessions. From her first entrance, Comare Maria Giuseppa talks nonstop about her family's wealth. When she first proposes that Maria Concezione marry her nephew Costante, habitually referred to by Deledda and her characters as *Costante lo scemo,* (the imbecile Costante), Maria Giuseppa frames the proposal with a virtuosic list of the "stuff" belonging to her house: cloth, jewels, all sorts of foodstuffs. From that point on, whenever Comare Maria Giuseppa appears, either she or another character will begin a litany to *la roba,* her "stuff."

La roba has more than a comic presence in this novel, it is also meant as a shorthand allusion to an attitude of worship of material things. The word itself is an echo of a famous short story by Giovanni Verga, first published in 1883.[27] This is the story of Mazzarò, a sly peasant who worked so long and hard that he eventually came to own everything that his former employers had: lands, orchards, animals, houses, all sorts of *roba.* These "possessions," (as D. H. Lawrence translates *la roba*) come to rule Mazzarò's life without ever letting him enjoy them. At the end of the story, when he realizes that he will have to die and that *la roba* will not come with him then, he explodes in a rage and storms through the barnyard, hitting his own ducks and geese and crying plaintively, "Roba mia, vientene con me!" ("My stuff, you come with me!").

Deledda and Verga were part of the same literary circle in Rome, and she certainly knew this famous collection of stories that included "Cavalleria rusticana," the basis for the Mascagni opera. Her portrait of Maria Giuseppa presents the same social problematic of the commodification of "stuff" described by Verga, but with some important differences. Maria Giuseppa is a woman of enormous appetites. Her appreciation of *la roba* is joyous, but she recognizes that she has more than she can ever use, and she is consumed by worries about who will inherit it. Comare Maria Giuseppa Alivia is the opposite of Aroldo the wandering troubadour. She is rooted in her stuff; her clinging to the things of this world provides an important foil to Maria Concezione, whose illness has made her so aware of her transient participation in the things of this earth.

The most obvious and lengthy reference to the Catholic faith shared by all of the characters in *La chiesa della solitudine* is an entire sermon preached by Serafino. Situated at the end of the first third of the novel, it functions as a first turning point in the tormented relationship between Concezione and Aroldo. Ironically, after hearing this sermon, overcome with jealousy even of the closeness between Concezione and the priest, Aroldo decides to buy a guitar from the local tavern owner. This is the beginning of his downfall.

The sermon begins with the story of a miraculous healing by Jesus as told in John 4:46–54. Here, the sick person healed is the son of a Roman Centurion; important elements of the story are the fact that Jesus never even has to see the boy, but only needs to pronounce him healed from afar, and the fact that the person who asks for a healing is not a follower of Jesus, in fact, is an enemy, a foreign *Regolo,* (ruler), as Serafino calls him. Other versions of this story, in which the person healed by Jesus is a servant or a slave rather than a son, are told in Matthew 5:8–13 and Luke 7:1–10, but the fact that Serafino chooses a family healing is very important.

Serafino's interpretation adds to the biblical narrative a description of a house, the new house just built by the ruler. This man had *la roba:* possessions, power, family; but then his young son sickened and seemed to be on the verge of death. In his desperation, the man asks Jesus, the "Rabbi with his miraculous claims," for help. The end of the story touches the theme of rebirth that is so important in the novel:

> "And the ruler also felt like he had been reborn into a new life; cured of the worst of all ills, the lack of faith. He seemed to be a lad again, like his beloved son, and to now be able to live an eternal youth, since he now believed in the word of God. And

when they heard his story, his family converted with him." (pp. 50–51)

Both Aroldo and Concezione immediately understand that the sermon was meant to touch Concezione spiritually, to lead her to a deeper belief in the will of God more than to lead her to expect a cure. But at the end of the novel, the newly resurrected Aroldo, still trembling from his brush with death, urges Concezione to think back to that sermon and be reassured that she will be healed. But Concezione has moved to another level of the interpretation of metaphors of sickness and health:

> "Yes, the boy was cured because Jesus wanted him to be. But then he also died, that boy; he's been dead for almost two thousand years, yet he still lives and plays alongside us. And we will also get well, Aroldo, with God's will, after our deaths. And now, listen, we need, in fact, to talk about eternal life." (p. 145)

La chiesa della solitudine ends with Maria Concezione alone, on her knees, in front of the Madonna della Solitudine. Deledda describes the spark in her eye that will still glow after her death, but she does not seem very close to death. Indeed, the fact that she made a vow to spend half of her inheritance to redecorate the little church if Aroldo were found safe suggests that by the end of the novel she is thinking about her future.

The ending of the novel is deliberately unresolved, but the issues are clear: the power of love, for God and for other people, to transcend the confines of *la roba* and offer redemption, and the strength that comes from solitude. The first part of this formula resonates with the central message of Christianity, while Deledda's emphasis on the individual strength of the protagonist, her unwillingness to accept definition by anyone else, seems almost feminist. Of course, this is not to say that Grazia Deledda was a "feminist author." In fact, she was clear about her apolitical stance; when once urged to take a stand on contemporary issues, she is reported to have answered, *"Io sono del passato"*

("I am of the past").[28] Perhaps it is possible, though, to understand *La chiesa della solitudine* as a "protofeminist" novel, because when we put down the book, it is the continuity of a woman's life that remains with us, even against the background of a patriarchally defined society.

In spite of the many references to Maria Concezione's bandit forefathers, she is never identified through them in the way that the Giordanos understand themselves as members of a patriarchal family ruled by old Felis, or possibly Serafino. We do not even know Concezione's family name. Her portrait, unlike those of Deledda's other autobiographical characters, Cosima and Nina, is of a woman who defines herself by her own experience, and who understands the power of solitude.

I would like to thank the John Simon Guggenheim Foundation and the R. Jean Brownlee Term Chair at the University of Pennsylvania for support of this project. Thanks also to Alessandro Madesani-Deledda, Grazia Deledda's grandson, for permission to publish this translation and to Diana Silverman for introducing me to Signor Madesani-Deledda. My work on this translation was a labor of love. I am especially grateful for the help and encouragement of friends who read over the manuscript with me, particularly Carla Locatelli, Diana Cavallo, Armando Maggi, Angela Locatelli, Neville Strumpf, Margaret Mills, and Robert Arbuckle. Many of their suggestions have been incorporated into the final translation. Any errors that remain are, of course, my responsibility.

Notes

1. Compare the half-column treatment (with photo) in the *New York Times* of August 17, 1936 (p. 19). It is noteworthy that Benito Mussolini is not reported to have sent condolences or made a public statement about Deledda's death, in contrast to his enthusiastic and frequent endorsements of other authors, especially Gabriele d'Annunzio and Luigi Pirandello. This laconic treatment in the *Corriere della sera* is especially striking since Deledda had been publishing regularly with the prestigious Milanese publishing house Treves since 1910.

2. *Nell'azzurro* (Milan-Rome: Trevisini, 1890).

3. *Cosima* (Milan: Treves, 1937). English translation by Martha King (New York: Italica Press, 1988).

4. *Dopo il divorzio* (Turin: Roux e Viaregno, 1902), republished as *Naufraghi in porto* (Milan: Treves, 1920), English translation *After the Divorce,* translated by Susan Ashe, with an introduction by Sheila MacLeod (London: Quartet Books, 1985); *Elias Portolu* (Turin: Roux e Viaregno, 1903), English translation by Martha King (London: Quartet Books, 1992); *Cenere* (Rome: Ripamonti e Colombo, 1904); *L'edera* (Rome: Colombi, 1910); *Canne al vento* (Milan: Treves, 1913), English translation by Martha King, with an introduction by Dolores Turchi; (New York: Italica Press, 1999).

5. Luigi Pirandello, *Suo marito* (Florence: Quattrini, 1911), English translation by Martha King, with an afterword by Martha King and Mary Ann Frese Witt (Durham [N.C.]: Duke University Press, 2000).

6. Luigi Pirandello, *Giustino Roncella nato Boggiòlo* (Milan: Mondadori, 1941).

7. Luigi Pirandello, *Suo marito,* edited by Laura Nay (Milan: Mondadori Oscar, 1994), p. 1. My translation. Deledda was in fact preparing several of her works for the stage and the cinema just when the first edition of *Suo marito* was published. See also the edition of Paola Brengola and Fabio Mantegazza (Milan: La Biblioteca Ideale Tascabile, 1995).

8. Lucio d'Ambra, "Il silenzio di Grazia Deledda. Ricordi della vita letteraria," *Corriere della sera* August 27, 1936, p. 3. My translation.

9. "Il Premio Nobel a Grazia Deledda," *Corriere della Sera* November 11, 1927, p. 3.

10. Grazia Deledda, *La chiesa della solitudine* (Milan: Treves, 1936); reprint Milano: Mondadori, 1956; fourth reprinting, Edizione Oscar Scrittori del Novecento, 1989, afterword by E. Ann Matter, 1999.

11. Carla Locatelli, "Premessa," in *I silenzi dei testi e i silenzi della critica* (Trent: Editrice Università degli Studi di Trento, 1996), p. 12. My translation. For a recent study of the power of silence in the works of another overlooked Italian woman writer, see Clotilde Barbarulli and Luciana Brandi, *I colori del silenzio. Strategie narrative e linguistiche in Maria Messina* (Ferrara: Tufani Editrice, 1996).

12. Anna Dolfi, *Grazia Deledda* (Milan: Mursia, 1979), p. 171. My translation. See the very similar paraphrasis in Dolfi's introduction to the new Oscar Scrittori del Novecento printing of *Il paese del vento* (Milan: Mondadori, 1994), p. 5.

13. Susan Sontag, *Illness as Metaphor* (New York: Farrar, Straus and Giroux, 1978), republished as *Illness as Metaphor and Aids and Its Metaphors* (New York: Anchor Books, 1990). All quotations are from the 1990 edition.

14. *Ibid.*, p. 9.

15. *Ibid.*, p. 3.

16. *Ibid.*, pp. 34–35.

17. *Ibid.*, pp. 23, 49.

18. *Il paese del vento* (Milan: Treves, 1931).

19. Anna Dolfi, "Introduzione," in the reprinting of Grazia Deledda, *Il paese del vento,* in the series Oscar Scrittori del Novecento (Milan: Mondadori, 1994), p. 9.

20. Dolores Turchi, "Introduzione," in Grazia Deledda, *Il paese del vento* (Rome: Newton Compton Editore, 1995), pp. 8–11. Deledda's letters to Manca are edited by Francesco Di Pilla in *Grazia Deledda, Premio Nobel 1926* (Milan: Fabbri, 1966), pp. 985–1019.

21. *Il paese del vento* (Milan: Mondadori, 1994) p. 91. My translation.

22. *Ibid.*, pp. 113–118.

23. Sontag, *Illness as Metaphor,* p. 53; see also pp. 48–49 for Auden's poem about "Miss Gee."

24. Compare descriptions of Serafino (p. 54–55) and the doctor (p. 83).

25. For love, see the story of the old woman and her bandit son (p. 140); for sex, the phlebotomist's frequent admonitions to Concezione (pp. 62, 84); for blood, his cure of Aroldo (pp. 146–147).

26. Renzo Rendi, "Grazia Deledda Wins the Nobel Prize," the *New York Times Book Review*, December 18, 1927, p. 2. The 1926 prize was not awarded until November, 1927.

27. Giovanni Verga, "La roba," in *Novelle rusticane* (Milan: Treves, 1883); current edition with an introduction by Carla Riccardi in Giovanni Verga, *Tutte le Novele*, vol. 1 (Milan: Mondadori, 1995), pp. 262–268; English translation of 1928 by D. H. Lawrence, "The Property," in *Short Sicilian Novels* (London: Daedalus, 1984), pp. 85–91.

28. "Grazia Deledda riceve dal Re di Svezia il Premio Nobel per la letteratura," *Corriere della sera,* December 11, 1927, p. 3.